The Curse
of the Horrible
Hair Day

Bethany House Books by
Bill Myers

Bloodhounds, Inc.
CHILDREN'S MYSTERY SERIES

The Ghost of KRZY
The Mystery of the Invisible Knight
Phantom of the Haunted Church
Invasion of the UFOs
Fangs for the Memories
The Case of the Missing Minds
The Secret of the Ghostly Hot Rod
I Want My Mummy
The Curse of the Horrible Hair Day

Nonfiction
The Dark Side of the Supernatural
Hot Topics, Tough Questions

Bill Myers' Web site: www.BillMyers.com

9

BloodHounds, INC.

The Curse of the Horrible Hair Day

Bill Myers

with DAVE WIMBISH

BETHANY HOUSE PUBLISHERS
MINNEAPOLIS, MINNESOTA 55438

The Curse of the Horrible Hair Day
Copyright © 2001
Bill Myers

Cover design by Lookout Design Group, Inc.

Published by Bethany House Publishers
A Ministry of Bethany Fellowship International
11400 Hampshire Avenue South
Bloomington, Minnesota 55438
www.bethanyhouse.com

Printed in the United States of America by
Bethany Press International, Bloomington, Minnesota 55438

Library of Congress Cataloging-in-Publication Data

CIP data applied for

ISBN 0-7642-2437-9

To Mark and Cindy,
who live the Bible's command
"Let us not be weary in well doing."

BILL MYERS is a youth worker, creative writer, and film director who co-created the "McGee and Me!" book and video series; his work has received over forty national and international awards. His many youth books include THE INCREDIBLE WORLDS OF WALLY MCDOOGLE series, his teen books: *Hot Topics, Tough Questions; Faith Encounter;* and *Forbidden Doors;* as well as his adult novels: *Eli,* and the trilogy *Blood of Heaven, Threshold,* and *Fire of Heaven.*

Contents

No weapon forged against you will prevail.

Isaiah 54:17

1

The Case Begins

FRIDAY, 19:30 PDST

BOOM...BOOM...BOOM...

The sound of the bass drum echoed through the crisp evening air.

"Yeaaah...!"

Sean and Melissa Hunter jumped to their feet, cheering loudly as the Midvale High School Tigers ran onto the football field.

"They look great, don't they?" Melissa shouted over the roar of the crowd.

"They sure do," Sean yelled back as he admired the team through his binoculars. "Brand-new uniforms, brand-new football field, brand-new everything. This is going to be a great year!"

"Over here, Dad," Melissa called down to her father, who shakily worked his way up the jam-packed bleachers.

In his hands he juggled six hot dogs (all for Sean), five pretzels (four for Sean), an extra-large bucket of popcorn (Melissa and Dad might get two handfuls if they were lucky), and three jumbo sodas.

"Hey, look out, pal! You're spilling that soda!"

"Sorry," Dad said as he continued to make his way up the bleachers.

"Here, Dad." Melissa reached out to him. "Let me help."

"Thanks, honey." He handed her the hot dogs. As she took them, a giant glob of mustard squished out and landed directly on top of the head of the woman in front of them, who just happened to be who else but Mrs. Tubbs. Fortunately, she didn't notice. Melissa quickly clapped her hand over her mouth and shot a look at Dad that asked, "Should I tell her?"

Dad wasn't sure. Normally he'd say yes, but Mrs. Tubbs, their cranky neighbor, had been in a particularly bad mood lately and seemed to be blaming the kids—and their huge bloodhound, Slobs—for everything.

Neither Sean nor Melissa thought it was fair. It wasn't their fault that Mrs. Tubbs managed to get involved in nearly every case their Bloodhounds, Inc. Detective Agency handled. It wasn't their fault that she'd been attacked by vampires, harassed by a ghostly hot rod, become involved in a crime spree with a renegade mummy, and chased all over town by a runaway robot. Well, all right, maybe it was a little of their fault, but at least nobody could say Mrs. Tubbs' life was boring!

As Dad sat down beside Melissa, she reached out with a napkin and tried dabbing the mustard out of Mrs. Tubbs' hair.

Mrs. Tubbs jerked around. "Did you want something?"

"No, ma'am," Melissa said. "I was just trying to—"

"Well, be careful!" Mrs. Tubbs scolded. "This hairdo cost me $200!"

"And will you be taking the hairdresser to *People's Court*?" Sean asked.

Melissa elbowed her brother in the ribs.

"Ooof!" he gasped.

"Pardon me?" Mrs. Tubbs shouted over the crowd.

"Uh . . ." Sean rubbed his ribs. "I just wanted to tell you that it was worth every penny!"

"Hmph!" Mrs. Tubbs replied haughtily as she turned her attention back to the football field. But as she turned, Melissa, Sean, and Dad gasped in unison. The big blob of mustard was now oozing down her head and toward her neck.

Melissa gave Dad a nervous look that said, "We've got to do something."

Dad nodded but just stared helplessly.

Finally feeling something, Mrs. Tubbs ran her fingers

through her hair . . . which only managed to smear the yellow mustard everywhere.

Now everyone could see the mess . . . including the woman beside Mrs. Tubbs. "Excuse me, ma'am," the woman said, pointing to Mrs. Tubbs' hair, "but I wondered if you knew—"

"You were wondering where I get my hair fixed?" Mrs. Tubbs asked proudly.

"Well, I . . . uh . . ."

"Beautiful, isn't it?" She carefully stroked her hair, streaking mustard in all directions.

"Well, uh . . . I . . ."

"I also use this wonderful styling gel," Mrs. Tubbs bragged, continuing to finger her hair. "It's called Lady Hairball. It's great, but very, very expensive."

"Expensive?" the lady cried. "It looks like you've got mustard in your—"

"Wow!" Dad shouted, trying to change the subject. He motioned down to the field, where the home team was warming up. "I haven't seen this much excitement in Midvale for . . . I don't know . . . twenty years!"

It worked. Mrs. Tubbs turned her attention back to the field. So did her neighbor.

"I tell you," Dad continued. "This brand-new high school is just what the doctor ordered for the town!"

"Yeah," Melissa agreed. "It's going to be great going to

school here in a couple years."

Sean shrugged. "I guess so." (Actually, he would have preferred the city to have spent all that money on a new skate park.)

"You'll be more excited about it next year when you're a freshman," Dad said. "The old high school was falling apart even when I went there twenty-fi—er, a few years back."

"Just think," Melissa added. "We'll have brand-new equipment in all the labs. New computers. New everything." She pointed across the football field, toward the new science building that sat, gleaming beautifully, in the moonlight. "It's really going to be cool going to school here!"

Sean shrugged again. Of course Melissa liked going to school. She always got A's. The only time Sean ever got an A was for recess, and that was way back in elementary school. Somehow he suspected a new school wasn't going to change that.

Down on the field, the Midvale High School principal approached the microphone to say a few words. Did I say "a few"? Actually, it took him fifteen minutes just to welcome everybody. I mean, the man went on and on, and just when you thought he'd finished, he went on some more. . . .

"And another thing I'd like to mention is—" Suddenly he stopped midsentence—actually, mid-word. A tall, thin woman wrapped in a white hooded robe strode out of the shadows and headed straight toward him. She had pulled up the collar on her robe so her face was barely visible. Dark sunglasses hid her eyes. And she didn't seem to be walking across the field.

It was more like floating.

Closer and closer she came as the principal stood there with his mouth hanging open, the microphone held limply in his hand.

The band came to a stop, and the crowd stirred audibly. Everyone waited to see what would happen. . . .

At last the hooded woman arrived. She grabbed the microphone from the principal's hand . . . or at least she tried to. Because if there was one thing greater than his shock, it was his love to talk. No way was he giving up the microphone that easily.

He had it!

No! She had it!

No! He had it!

Finally, with one mighty yank, the mysterious woman grabbed the mike and sent the principal staggering into the players' bench. She raised a bony finger and pointed it at the crowd. As she spoke she turned in a circle, covering the entire football field with her gesture.

"You have desecrated this land!" Her voice trembled with anger. "Look around you! Everything you see is sacred to my ancestors. For generations it has been our holy place! But now"—she swept her hand in front of her—"you have polluted it with these profane buildings and this field of play."

Sean and Melissa exchanged nervous glances. Sean raised his binoculars to get a better look.

The woman continued, "Because of what you have done, from this day forward, this school will be cursed."

She gestured toward the Midvale Tigers. "This football team will be cursed."

She pointed at the bleachers. "Everyone who came to the game tonight will be cursed." Her voice grew more and more shrill. "In fact, this entire town will be cursed!"

By now the principal had staggered back to his feet. But she was finished and handed the microphone back to him with a surprisingly polite "Thank you." Then she turned and strode off the field into the darkness.

Sean followed the woman through the binoculars as she walked away. A stiff autumn breeze swirled across the field, causing her hood to fall away for just a moment before she pulled it back on.

What was that on the back of her neck? Sean wondered. *A spider. Some kind of tattoo?*

As he pondered the question, an eerie silence settled over the stadium. Suddenly the principal began to chuckle. Soon he was laughing hard. And sooner still, members of the crowd started laughing right along with him.

Finally, he turned and pointed his finger toward the opposing team's bench. "Nice joke, boys!" he laughed. "But we're not falling for it!"

The other team's coach raised his hands as if to say, "I don't know what you're talking about." But the principal didn't seem to believe him.

"Curse schmurse!" the principal shouted good-naturedly. "It will take more than a curse to beat the Midvale Tigers!"

The crowd began to cheer.

"I don't understand," Melissa said to Dad. "Why would the other team want us to think we've been cursed?"

"Because they're the Rockport Rangers, our biggest rival," Dad explained.

"But what does that—"

"You know," Sean interrupted. "Every year they try to do things to psych us out. They come over and steal our mascot, or we go over to Rockport and steal their mascot, or—"

Melissa shook her head. "It all seems kind of stupid to me. Why don't we just play football?"

Dad put his arm around her. "This has been going on for years, honey," he said. "And it's not likely to stop anytime soon. Oh, it's time for the kickoff!"

The crowd stood to its feet.

The referee raised his arm and blew his whistle. Someone in the band began doing a drum roll to build the tension. The Rockport kicker approached the ball and . . .

K-BAMB!

. . . booted a beautiful kick. It spiraled high and deep toward Midvale's star receiver, who waited anxiously in front of his own end zone.

He caught the ball and the crowd cheered.

Melissa gasped and closed her eyes as a trio of Rockport players charged in for the tackle. But when she opened her eyes, she saw three Rockport players falling to the ground as the Midvale player jitterbugged his way past them, then zoomed down the sideline.

He was at his own thirty . . . thirty-five . . . forty . . . and picking up speed!

Someone lunged for him, but he zigged left.

Another lunged for him, and he zagged right.

The crowd screamed wildly.

Just twenty more yards for a Midvale touchdown! It looked like a sure six points for the Tigers. When suddenly . . .

His pants fell down!

That's right. We're not talking a little slippage here. We're not even talking down to the knees. We're talking

17

about a major falling all the way down to his ankles—which, of course, caused him to trip and do a nose dive into the grass.

Even that wouldn't have been so bad, except that the football popped out of his arms and flew high into the air. The good news was a group of Midvale players grabbed for it. The bad news was they only succeeded in batting it back into the air.

This time it came down straight into the arms of a Rockport defender. He hugged the ball close and sprinted eighty yards, all the way back to Rockport's end zone.

While all this was going on, the Midvale cheerleaders had been in the middle of performing one of their most exciting routines, "The Pyramid of Power." But suddenly the girl on top lost her footing.

"Whoah . . . oh . . . look out!"

The entire pyramid collapsed like a house of cards, spilling cheerleaders everywhere. Fortunately, it looked like nobody was hurt.

Then, before the embarrassed cheerleaders could even pick themselves up, a voice shouted, "Fire! Fire!"

Everyone turned to see smoke pouring out of the concession stand windows. The entire snack bar was burning.

"What's going on?" Melissa shouted. "What's happening?!"

Two hours later, the crowd of Midvale fans slowly made its way out of the stadium.

"I can't believe it," Sean said, shaking his head. "Sixty-three to nothing! And I thought we had a good team this year."

"Me too," Dad said.

Melissa pulled herself closer to her father. "Do you hear what everyone is saying?"

He nodded. "They're talking about the curse. They think maybe it's for real."

Sean shrugged. "Well, maybe it is."

"There's no such thing as a curse," his father reminded him.

"But, Dad," Melissa said, "sixty-three to nothing. And the cheerleaders falling, and the concession stand burning down."

"And don't forget the drum major who got his head stuck in the tuba during the half-time show," Sean said. "Though that *was* pretty cool."

"Or the referee who sprained his ankle," Melissa added.

Dad shook his head. "First-game jitters, that's all. Or maybe that curse thing got everybody all shook up. But I'll say it again, guys. There's no such thing as a curse. And anybody who believes otherwise is—*WHOOPS!*"

Suddenly Dad was flying through the air and landing on his rear.

"Dad, are you all right?" Melissa and Sean bent down to help him up.

"Sure . . . sure," he said, struggling to his feet. "Just slipped on some mustard." He looked at the bottom of his shoe. "But there's no curse!"

"Sure, Dad," Sean said gravely. "No curse." But as his eyes met Melissa's, each knew what the other was thinking: *Maybe there is and maybe there isn't. . . .*

2

The Curse Continues

MONDAY, 14:55 PDST

SHOOOP...SHOOOP...SHOOOP...

Hildagard Tubbs waddled across her living room. As she did, her furry bunny slippers made soft slapping noises on the plush carpet.

She pulled back the corner of one of her thick green draperies and peered out the window. "Hmm," she said. The world hadn't fallen apart. Not yet, at least. But she wasn't about to take any chances. She glared in the direction of Sean and Melissa's house and slowly ran her fingers through her hair. "I wonder where all that mustard came from?" And then, snarling, she added, "As if I didn't know."

"Meowwrrr!"

Precious, her beloved Persian cat—who, if not for his color and fur could be mistaken for a very large watermelon—sat staring into his empty food dish.

"I know, I know," Mrs. Tubbs said. "I'm hungry, too. But I don't have a single bite of food in the house. And I'm not going out there . . . at least until I know if it's safe or not."

She reached into her housecoat pocket and started rubbing her rabbit's foot. There, that made her feel better. Then there was her laminated four-leaf clover that rested in her other pocket. And the "lucky penny" that dangled from a chain around her neck.

I guess I'll be okay, she thought. *I mean, as long as I have all my good-luck charms.*

After another moment of building up her courage, Mrs. Tubbs turned to her cat. "Come on, Precious," she said. "Let's go for a ride."

SHOOOP . . . SHOOOP . . . SHOOOP!

She padded across the floor to where Precious (who is not the smartest cat in this world) remained staring into his food dish, as if he expected the Meow Mix to suddenly appear.

She bent down to pick him up and . . .

ZZZZAAP!

. . . sparks of static electricity suddenly filled the air.

Suddenly Mrs. Tubbs' hair was standing up on top of her head.

Suddenly Precious's fur was standing up all over his body.

Suddenly both of them looked like porcupines.

Precious howled and ran straight for the bedroom, where he scrambled for safety under Mrs. Tubbs' bed. But since he's not the brightest of animals, he forgot that he didn't fit and got himself stuck halfway in and halfway out.

And Mrs. Tubbs, not being the brightest of owners, dropped to her knees and tried to rescue him. Unfortunately, since she was bigger than Precious, that meant—you guessed it—she also got stuck.

MONDAY, 15:25 PDST

"Hey, where you going?" Melissa called after her brother. "Dad told us to go straight to the radio station after school."

"Yeah, yeah," Sean answered. "I thought maybe we could just go by the football field for a minute . . . you know, to watch the guys practice."

Melissa folded her arms and shook her head. (When it came to Sean, it seems she was always folding her arms and shaking her head.) "Dad wanted to take us to a late lunch," she said.

"Don't bet on it," Sean answered. "With all those sunspots happening, he's probably still working on the equipment."

Melissa reluctantly agreed. Dad had said the solar activity was really breaking up the station's transmission. Besides, it seemed ever since their mother had died, Dad spent more and more time at the station and less and less time at home. Their aunt had said not to worry, that sometimes that's how men handle pain. It's not that he wasn't a good father; he was great. But sometimes he got to missing their mother so badly that he would try to forget his loneliness by keeping himself busy at work. Melissa knew he missed her—maybe more than she did. She would never forget that night when she got up to get a drink of water and caught him sitting at the kitchen table, quietly crying.

"Five minutes," Sean said. "I just want to see if, you know, they're, uh . . ."

Melissa shook her head. "You want to see if they're really under a curse, don't you?"

"Of course not," Sean protested. "That would be stupid."

Melissa gave him a look.

"Well, all right," he admitted. "Maybe I do. But it will only be for five minutes."

Reluctantly, Melissa agreed. They'd barely started for

the practice field before Sean said, "Sis, let me see your hand a second."

She gave him a dubious look.

"Come on," he said.

Expecting to be the victim of one of his practical jokes, Melissa gave a heavy sigh and held out her hand. He took it and rubbed it against his cheek.

"Feel that?" he asked.

"Feel what?" she said. "You getting a zit or something?"

"No, it's a whisker. Maybe even two. I think I need a shave!"

Melissa pulled her hand away. "Sorry, Sean, I don't feel any whiskers."

"But I felt one this morning," he argued.

"Well, it's gone now. Maybe it fell off."

Suddenly he looked very sad.

"Sorry," she said. "I know you want to grow a goatee like the college kids, but you're not quite there yet."

Sean scowled, rubbing his chin. "I was sure it was a whisker," he grumbled.

By the time they arrived at the football field, practice was in full swing.

First they watched the kicker practicing his field goals. He looked to be in perfect form as he ran up to kick the ball. But at the last second . . .

SWOOOOSH!

. . . his feet went out from under him, and . . .

BAMB!

. . . he landed flat on his back without even touching the ball.

On the far side of the field, the team's punt returner was practicing catching kicks. He waved his arms as he circled under a punt, ready to make a catch. But suddenly he seemed to lose the ball in the sun and it . . .

KER-PLUNK!

. . . bounced off the top of his head, sending him sprawling to the ground.

Sean and Melissa sat on the bleachers, heads in their hands, watching in disbelief.

"This is terrible!" Sean exclaimed.

"They're even worse today than they were Friday," Melissa agreed.

"You can say that again," someone said.

They turned to see the football coach, Ray Nelson, leaning against the wire-mesh fence, slowly shaking his head.

"I'm sorry, Coach," Melissa apologized. "I didn't mean to be critical."

"It's all right." He continued to shake his head. "They really are terrible."

"What happened?" Sean asked. "Everyone said they were so good before."

The coach sighed. "I think it's because they're all buying into that stupid curse."

He pointed to the middle of the field, where the players were practicing passing patterns. The quarterback threw the ball perfectly . . . but it zipped right through the receiver's hands and . . .

K-THUNK!

. . . hit him square in the mouth.

"I can't convince them that it was just a joke!" Coach Nelson said. "So they're playing like this. Hey, wait a minute." He pointed to them. "Didn't I see you kids on TV—something about that mummy?"

"That's right," Sean grinned. "We're—"

"Now I remember. You're those detective kids. Hound Dogs, Unlimited."

"Uh, actually, that's Bloodhounds, Incorporated," Melissa corrected.

"Whatever." The coach turned and watched his center hike the ball five feet over the quarterback's head. Suddenly he turned back to them. "Hey, listen, I've got an idea."

Sean and Melissa both looked at him.

"What if I hire you two to find the woman who put

that curse on Midvale and get her to take it off."

Sean and Melissa exchanged glances.

The coach continued, growing more excited. "I'll pay you any amount you want."

Sean raised an eyebrow. "Any amount?"

"That's right, any amount," Coach Nelson repeated. "Just get this curse off of my team, and I'll pay any price!"

Out on the field, the quarterback threw another pass. Or at least he tried to. But the ball slipped out of his hand and bounced harmlessly to the turf.

Coach Nelson buried his head in his hands, no longer able to watch.

Melissa did the same. It was just too painful.

But not for Sean. He was still focused on the words *any amount*.

"All right, Coach," he exclaimed. "You got yourself a deal!"

The coach looked up, his eyes brightening. "You mean it?"

"Yes, sir."

"Oh, thank you," the big man said. And for a moment it almost looked like he was going to cry. "Thank you, thank you . . ."

"Come on, sis," Sean said, his chest obviously swelling about ten sizes. "We've got a case to solve."

MONDAY, 16:15 PDST

Mrs. Tubbs gripped the steering wheel with both hands as her heart pounded wildly in her chest.

So far, so good. Only two more blocks and they'd make it to Ramsey's Market.

Precious sat on the seat beside her, looking almost as nervous as she did.

Mrs. Tubbs breathed a sigh of relief as she slowly eased her 1963 Studebaker into Ramsey's parking lot. A moment later, she'd found a parking spot. She thrust her hand into her sweater pocket to make certain she still had all of her good-luck charms.

"Good," she sighed, "very good." Then, turning to Precious, she said, "Okay, sweetie-weetie. You wait wight here, and Mommy will be wight back, otay?"

"Meowr," Precious said, sounding as sweet and cute as an ugly thirty-five-pound cat can sound.

Mrs. Tubbs gave him a little kiss on the head, then turned and climbed out of her car. She'd barely stepped away before a man shouted, "Hey, lady! Is that your car?"

"Why, yes," she said proudly. "It's a classic."

"Maybe," he answered. "But it's rolling toward the street!"

"What?!" Mrs. Tubbs spun around and screamed. The man was right. Her car was picking up speed, rolling down the steep parking lot into the street. From inside, poor Precious was frantically clawing at the windshield, his eyes wide with terror, as the car rolled faster and faster.

Mrs. Tubbs took off after the vehicle, screaming all the while, "Help me! Help me! Somebody save my baby!"

"Did you hear that?" a woman shopper shouted. "There's a baby in that car!"

One of the bag boys who had been collecting shopping carts saw what was happening and started after the car. But it was no use. By now it was zooming at at least twenty miles an hour. There was no way anyone could catch it.

After a few more steps and a lot more screaming, Mrs. Tubbs finally bent over with her hands on her knees, panting for breath. "I put the brake on," she gasped. "I know I did, I know I did. It's got to be the curse. I tell you, it's got to be the curse!"

Meanwhile, the Studebaker continued picking up speed.

WHAP!

There went the "Welcome to Ramsey's Market" sign.

Fortunately, the front tires just missed the beautiful roadside petunias. Unfortunately . . .

KEE-RUNCH!

. . . the back tires didn't.

Now the car was on the main street and rapidly picking up speed . . . as poor Precious clawed frantically at the windshield, meowing for help.

Still gasping for air, Mrs. Tubbs resumed the chase, all the time screaming about her baby.

Not too far down the hill, a city maintenance worker was repainting the white line along the middle of Main Street. His mind was completely on his work as he bent over, painting as carefully as a man could possibly paint. Then he heard it. The approaching car.

(And the screaming. Lots and lots of screaming.)

He looked up and saw Mrs. Tubbs' car heading straight for him. It was twenty feet away and closing in fast! And just as frightening as seeing the approaching car was seeing the driver.

A cat?! A crazy killer cat was driving the car. And it wanted to run him down! The painter could see its yellow eyes glaring at him, the awful, twisted grin on its face.

He darted to the left, but the car kept right on coming.

He darted to the right.

And still the car came.

Soon he was running back and forth and forth and back, spilling paint in all directions. But nothing he did seemed to do any good. The cat was still bearing down upon him.

Then, at the last second, the man leaped onto the sidewalk and the car whizzed past, missing him by THAT much . . . and causing him to leave paint all over the road.

Meanwhile, Sean and Melissa were walking down Fourth Street toward the radio station. They were in deep conversation over what they'd seen at the football field when they started to cross the intersection of Fourth and Main. That's when they heard the commotion and looked up just in time to see Mrs. Tubbs' sedan barreling toward them.

"Look out!" Melissa screamed. She grabbed her brother and pulled him toward the curb. In fact, she jerked him so hard that his backpack tumbled onto the street. Right under the left front tire . . .

KA-THUMP!

. . . of the speeding Studebaker. The car swerved slightly, bouncing up onto the sidewalk and speeding across the courthouse lawn, where . . .

KA-BLAM!

. . . it plowed into the bronze statue of the town's founder, Mortimer Muffinhoffer, and his trusty horse, Shirley. Here, at last, it came to a stop as . . .

SSSSHH . . .

32

. . . air gushed out of a couple of its tires.

But at least the car had stopped moving and Precious's wild ride had ended. Unfortunately, the same could *not* be said for Mortimer Muffinhoffer. He teetered back and forth on ol' Shirley until he did a swan dive . . .

KER-WHAM!

. . . right onto the roof of Mrs. Tubbs' car.

Her classic was a classic no more.

The bag boy from Ramsey's Market was the first to reach the scene. He was followed by Sean and Melissa, then what must have been half the population of Midvale—until Mrs. Tubbs finally broke through the crowd, huffing, puffing, and, of course, continuing to scream, "My baby! My baby! My baby!"

"Don't worry, ma'am," the bag boy cried. "I'll save your baby!" He reached the driver's door and jerked it open to meet . . .

MEOWRRRRRR!

. . . one very frightened cat. Precious leaped out of the car and on top of the kid's head, digging in his claws.

"Yiiiii!" the kid screamed. "Get it off! Get it off me!" He spun in circles into the street, but Precious would not let go. In fact, the cat might still be stuck to the poor kid's head if Mrs. Tubbs hadn't raced to him.

"My baby!" she cried, holding out her arms to her

precious Precious. "My baby! My baby!" Until the cat finally jumped to her.

"Are you getting all of this?" someone shouted.

Sean and Melissa turned. "Oh no," Melissa groaned. And for good reason. It was TV reporter Rafael Ruelas, yelling to his cameraman. Rafael Ruelas, the world's biggest exaggerator and worst reporter.

He raced up to Mrs. Tubbs and thrust his microphone into her face.

"What happened?" he shouted.

"It . . . it was the curse!" she cried. "I mean, I had the brake on. I had the car in park. There's no way it could have rolled down the street unless . . ."

A murmur spread through the crowd. Melissa couldn't hear everything they said, but she did hear the word "curse" spoken over and over again, plus comments like:

"I seen a ghost or somethin' pushin' that car down the street!" someone shouted.

"And I heard a weird noise," another volunteered. "You know . . . like . . . *whoooooooooooo!*"

Mrs. Tubbs nodded in agreement. "Yes, of course it was the curse! I could feel an evil presence in that car. And if we don't do something fast, this whole town may be doomed!"

Rafael Ruelas pulled the microphone back and stared

into the camera. "Doomed," he repeated. "Wise words from a wise woman."

But Melissa could no longer contain herself. "There's no such thing as a curse!" she shouted. "Curses don't exist!"

"You tell that to Mortimer Muffinhoffer," a nearby observer said, pointing to the toppled statue.

"Or to that cat," another said.

"Or to this whole town," a third agreed.

MONDAY, 16:35 PDST

"Hey, guys!" Herbie, KRZY's clumsy engineer, looked up from his work as the kids walked through the doors of the radio station.

"What did you do this time?" Melissa asked.

"Oh, this?" Herbie asked, referring to the scrapes and bruises covering his body and the heavy bandages wrapped around his right hand. "I . . . uh, well . . . I had a little accident at the bowling alley."

"Bowling alley?" Sean asked. "What happened?"

"Well . . . I got a new ball, you see . . . and I think maybe I had 'em drill the finger holes a little bit too small."

"And . . ." Sean asked, knowing there was more.

"And when I went to bowl, it wouldn't come off my hand and it kinda dragged me all the way down the alley!" He closed his eyes, slowly shaking his head at the painful memory. "But that wasn't nearly as bad as when the automatic ball return picked us up and pulled us all the way back."

Sean threw a look to Melissa, who could only roll her eyes.

"Your dad is in the control room," Herbie said, pointing to the glass-enclosed booth. "He's wrapping up the afternoon call-in show."

The kids caught Dad's attention through the glass and gave a wave. He nodded to them as he answered what was to be the last call of the day.

"You're on the air," he said. "What's on your mind?"

"I wasn't kidding," the voice on the other end replied.

Sean tilted his head. He'd heard that voice somewhere before. But where?

"Kidding?" Dad asked. "Kidding about what?"

"About the curse."

Sean snapped his fingers. Of course, at the football game! That's where he'd heard it. The voice belonged to the woman who had pronounced the so-called curse upon Midvale!

"The curse is real!" she said. "And if the new high

school is not torn down immediately, this town is doomed—along with everyone who lives here."

"I see," Dad answered. "And who exactly are—"

But before he could finish, there was a loud click. And then nothing but a dial tone . . .

3

It Can't Get Any Worse Than This

(. . . or can it?)

SATURDAY, 9:30 PDST

The little fellow was disturbed. He was distraught. He was agitated.

TRANSLATION: He was a little bugged.

His face, which was usually a healthy shade of green, had turned deep purple. Recklessly, he threw shirts and slacks into his glowing suitcase.

"Jeremiah," Sean asked, "what are you doing?"

"What does it look like I'm doing?" he said. "I'm kicking the road."

"Hitting," Sean corrected. "*Hitting* the road."

The little guy looked up from the face of Sean's digital wristwatch and shrugged. "Any way you want to say it,

I'm low-tailing it out of here."

"High-tailing," Melissa said as she peered over her brother's shoulder. "But why?"

Jeremiah shuddered. "Because we're all over a curse. That's why!"

"You mean *under* a curse?" Melissa asked.

"That's right," Jeremiah said as he snapped his suitcase shut. "This town is dumbed. . . ."

"Doomed," Sean corrected.

"See," Jeremiah said. "He believes it, too."

Jeremiah—which, as you probably know by now, stands for Johnson Electronic Reductive Entity Memory Inductive Assembly Housing—isn't a real person, but he doesn't seem to know that. He is an invention of the kids' scientist friend, Doc. Doc can't speak or hear, but that doesn't keep her from being the smartest person the kids have ever met.

Doc has invented a number of amazing things. A holographic camera, a jet engine the size of a pencil sharpener, a "thinking cap" that increases a person's intelligence by four hundred percent, and robots that can do an entire day's worth of chores in ten minutes flat. (And destroy an entire neighborhood in less than five!)

But as far as Sean and Melissa were concerned, Jeremiah—Doc's first invention—was still her best invention. Even though Jeremiah is completely electrical energy, he has his own personality and intelligence. But ever since that explosion in the fortune-cookie factory (don't ask, it's a long story), he tends to get his sayings mixed up a bit. He spends lots of his time in Sean's digital watch. But sometimes he shows up on computer games, or television sets . . . and when the power is really flowing, sometimes he's even able to briefly become a part of the "real world."

When that happens, look out! It means trouble is definitely on the way!

"Come on, Jeremiah," Melissa scolded. "You know there's no such thing as a curse."

"Oh yeah?" The little guy had turned purple again. "After what's gone on in this town during the last week, nobody's gonna tell me there's no such thing as a curse! Watch this!"

In a flash he disappeared from Sean's watch, and a video-taped replay of the latest football game—an away game between Midvale High and the Northfield Tree Frogs appeared.

The Midvale team waited for the opening kickoff.

The referee stood off to the side with his arm raised in the air, ready to give the signal that would start the game.

TWEEET!

He blew his whistle, gave a chopping motion with his

arm, and the Midvale kicker ran at the ball.

WHAAAPP!

He kicked the ball hard. . . .

Unfortunately, it didn't fly down the field toward the other team's receivers. Instead, it went sideways and . . .

WHAMM!

. . . smashed into the referee's face, which caused him to . . .

GULPPP!
GAAAACK!

. . . swallow his whistle. The poor guy managed to scramble to his feet as the opposing team scooped up the ball (which had come to rest on the fifteen-yard line) and ran it into the end zone for a touchdown.

The referee raised his arms over his head and tried to shout the word "touchdown." At least, it looked like that was what he was shouting. It was hard to tell with nothing but whistling noises coming from his mouth.

And from there things just got worse. Let's skip the gory details and just say that by the time they were in the fourth quarter the score was fifty-six to three. (And you don't have to be a genius to figure who had the three.)

This time, the Midvale quarterback dropped back to pass. He threw the ball beautifully. Unfortunately, his receiver forgot to turn around and look for it and . . .

K-POW!

. . . the ball hit him on the back of his head. It popped up into the air and into the hands of an opposing defender who . . . you guessed it . . . ran it all the way back for another touchdown.

Sean could only stare and let out a groan.

"Seen enough?" the little voice chirped from his wrist. Now Jeremiah was standing in his watch, suitcase in hand. "I'm telling you it has to be the curse."

Sean let out a heavy sigh. "I don't think the Midvale team could be that bad even if they tried."

"That's what I mean," Jeremiah said as he turned and started walking away. "Like I said, I'm outta here. See you a square."

"Around," Sean called after him. "The phrase is 'See you around.'"

But Jeremiah didn't reply. Instead, he just kept growing smaller and smaller on the screen until he disappeared altogether.

Meanwhile, in a darkened room halfway across town, a key turned in a lock and a door creaked open.

A tall, slender woman entered. She closed the door and locked it. She clicked on a small lamp that sat atop a cherrywood desk. Then she slipped into the chair behind the desk, leaned back, and sighed contentedly.

She opened the top drawer of the desk, rummaged around inside, then pulled out a black notebook and began to write:

> *Things are going even better than I had hoped. The whole town seems to be falling apart.*

She hesitated and looked up for a moment. And then she resumed writing:

> *Sometimes I almost feel sorry for them.*

"That's ridiculous," she mumbled as she continued to write.

> *Why should I feel sorry for anybody? They'll only get what they deserve. And so will I.*

At last the woman set down the notebook and reached over to snap off the light. Then, in the darkness of the room, she added, "And when I do . . . everybody will know my name. *Everybody!*"

44

SATURDAY, 10:20 PDST

Sean and Melissa had no clues. It had been over a week since the curse had been spoken, and they still had no leads. They had no idea where to start. How do you go about tracking down curses . . . especially if you don't even believe they exist?

So they decided to do what they always do when they run out of ideas. They went to see Doc. After all, she seemed to know just about everything about everything. Maybe she could shed some light on this "curse" business.

They found her in her workshop, making improvements to her holographic video camera, the very one they had used in *Invasion of the UFOs*.

In the background, a television was tuned to Channel 34, where Rafael Ruelas was doing his usual ranting and raving.

Good morning, Melissa gestured to Doc in sign language.

Morning, Doc signed back. *What's up?*

Sean stepped up to the small keyboard and monitor they often used for communicating and typed, *We're just wondering what you know about curses.*

Curses? Doc typed. *Not much. Except that they don't exist.*

Are you sure? Melissa signed.

Doc thought for a moment, then typed, *I have heard of instances where people got sick and even died because they thought they were under a curse. But that doesn't mean the curse was real.*

Melissa shrugged. *It doesn't?*

No, Doc typed. *It just shows the power of the human mind. If you think bad things are going to happen to you, they probably will. However—*

Suddenly the screen went blank and . . .

"Jeremiah!" Sean shouted as the little guy flashed on the monitor. "You've come back!"

"I forgot my toothbrush," he said. "Gotta keep my teeth a nice bright green, you know."

Melissa wanted to remind him that electronically generated images didn't have any teeth, but she decided it would be best not to hurt his feelings.

Meanwhile, over on the TV in the corner, Rafael Ruelas was interviewing the mayor of Midvale, who kept arguing with him.

"No, Rafael, I do not believe there is a curse. True, there have been some minor instances around town, and yes, we had quite a violent rainstorm during the night and it's done some damage to a few of the businesses downtown. But that is no reason to believe . . . to believe . . ." The mayor hesitated, taking a shaky breath. It looked like he was going to sneeze. "To belie—"

Suddenly he let loose a powerful sneeze . . . the likes of which Sean and Melissa had never seen before.

AAAHHHH—CHOOOOO!

In fact, he sneezed so hard that he blew his false teeth right out of his head. One minute they were bright and gleaming in his mouth. The next they were shooting from his face like a rocket. But even that wouldn't have been so bad if they hadn't landed directly on the front of Rafael's shirt.

"Ick!" Rafael cried. "Get 'em off! Get 'em off!"

Unfortunately, in his desperation to get free of them, Mr. Ruelas leaped backward until he . . .

ZZZTTTTTTT!

. . . stepped into a giant puddle left by last night's rain.

Electricity surged from the microphone he was holding and into his body. He began to shake, shiver, and dance.

And if anyone had been looking at Jeremiah, they would have seen that he, too, was starting to shiver. Being made entirely of electricity, it was obvious Jeremiah was really relating to Rafael's own shocking experience.

Back on TV, Ruelas's hair began to smoke. The mayor reached up and began swatting it, trying to put out the fire. But as he did, his fingers got tangled in Ruelas's hair, and he lifted it right off his head!

Wait a minute, it wasn't hair at all. It was a wig!

Rafael Ruelas was completely bald!

Meanwhile, Jeremiah continued to grow brighter and brighter. Sparks began shooting off from his body. What was going on? What was happening to him? What was—

KA-POW!

An explosion filled the TV screen. And suddenly, standing there, where Rafael Ruelas had been, was . . .

Jeremiah! He stood in all his green glory with a bewildered look on his face. And in his hands was the microphone!

The shocked mayor leaped backward, dropping Rafael Ruelas's wig sideways on top of Jeremiah's head when, suddenly . . .

KA-POW!

. . . there was another explosion, and the entire picture disappeared.

Now there was only a test pattern and a high-pitched whistling sound.

In the lab, Melissa clasped her hand over her mouth. "Did you see that?" she gasped.

"I sure did," Sean answered. "And I'm shocked. Who would have believed that Rafael Ruelas wore a wig?"

4

I Don't Believe in Curses!
(...but has anyone seen my lucky rabbit's foot?)

SUNDAY, 8:15 PDST

Sunday morning is always a little hectic in the Hunter household.

Did I say "a little"? Better make that a lot. . . .

On this particular morning, Dad was trying to get a quick look at the Sunday paper while shaving, polishing his shoes, and tying his tie . . . all at the same time.

Sean was frantically searching the house for his Bible, the same thing he does every Sunday morning before Sunday school. Of course, it might be a little easier if he actually looked at the book some other time during the week. But that would mean reading, and reading has never been his strong point.

"Dad," he suddenly cried, "what's that smell? Did somebody scare a skunk?"

Dad motioned toward the kitchen. "Your sister's fixing breakfast."

"What . . . again?" Sean groaned. "Dad, you know she shouldn't—"

"She's turning into quite a good little cook," Dad said. "And I'd appreciate it if you would try to give her a little encouragement."

"What? You mean like actually eating the stuff she makes?" Sean shuddered at the thought.

"Well, uh . . . sure," Dad answered. "I mean . . . if you can."

"That's a big 'if,' " Sean said.

Dad nodded in understanding, then decided to change the subject. "So, Coach Nelson wants to hire you guys?"

"Yup. Had us go to his office yesterday so we could look at films of Friday night's game. What a disaster!"

Dad sighed. "I've talked to three or four families in the last week who've told me they're thinking about moving out of Midvale. What a shame. All over a little prank."

"It's more than a prank," Sean said. "I mean, the stuff that's happening in this town is just crazy! And dangerous!"

Dad shook his head. "Well, whatever's going on here,

it's not because of some curse. And even if it were, you two wouldn't have to worry."

"Why do you say that?"

"The Bible says that 'No weapon forged against you will prevail.' "

"Meaning?" Sean asked.

"Meaning that—"

"EEEEEEEE!!"

The scream came from the kitchen. Immediately Sean and Dad raced down the stairs to Melissa's rescue. When they arrived, they saw her bent over the sink, choking and gagging. And for good reason. Her necklace was caught in the whirring garbage disposal! She couldn't reach the Off switch, and the disposal kept pulling her down . . . down . . . down!

Dad lunged for the switch, but before he could turn it off, the necklace broke, and Melissa staggered backward across the kitchen. Which might have been a good thing, except for . . .

"LOOK OUT!" Sean cried.

Too late. She fell across the stove, which immediately caught the back of her blouse on fire. Thinking fast, Sean grabbed the sink hose and . . .

SSSSSSSTTTTT . . .

. . . dowsed his sister.

The good news was he put out the fire. The bad news was he got it in her eyes, which caused her to wave her arms in self-defense and . . .

KER-SPLAT!

. . . knock a skillet full of greasy scrambled eggs onto the floor. Which, in turn . . .

"WHOA! LOOK OUT!"

. . . caused Sean to go slipping and sliding across the kitchen floor. He grabbed the tablecloth in an attempt to keep from falling, but it didn't work. Instead, he . . .

THUMP!

. . . sat down *hard* on the kitchen floor. Even that wouldn't have been so bad if he'd remembered to let go of the tablecloth. But he didn't, which, of course, meant both it and the breakfast dishes . . .

KER-ASH! TINKLE! TINKLE! TINKLE!

. . . fell down on his head.

Slobs, the kids' huge bloodhound, thought this was great fun. She raced into the kitchen, barking and running around in circles, slurping up the scrambled eggs (no doubt hoping Melissa would throw bacon down on the floor, as well).

But the dishes were still falling on Sean, right along with . . .

K-PLOP! K-PLOP! K-PLOP!

. . . the stack of pancakes. And what good were pancakes without . . .

GLUG! GLUG! GLUG!

. . . you guessed it—syrup. Lots and lots of syrup.

At last the catastrophe was over. For the longest moment Sean just sort of sat there in a daze as Slobs ate the pancakes off his head and licked the syrup dribbling down his face.

When Melissa saw that her Sunday morning breakfast had turned into the biggest disaster since . . . well, since last Sunday's disaster, she raced from the kitchen in tears and bounded up the stairs to her room.

"Don't cry, Melissa," Dad called as he stooped down to his son. "I can tell it would have been delicious!"

But instead of answering, Melissa . . .

WHAM!

. . . slammed her bedroom door.

"Really!" Dad shouted back. "Slobs loves it!"

WHAM! WHAM!

Apparently she opened and slammed her door twice more, just to make it clear how upset she was.

"Unbelievable," Dad said as he helped Sean to his feet. "Are you okay, son?"

"Yeah," Sean muttered. "I'll be all right."

"Are you sure? A couple of those dishes whacked you pretty hard. And you've got pancakes and syrup all over your head."

Sean nodded, picking off the pieces and handing them to Slobs. "I'll tell you something." He glanced up the stairs and lowered his voice so he wouldn't be heard.

"What's that?"

"When it comes to her cooking . . . I'd rather be wearing it than eating it."

SUNDAY, 14:15 PDST

Melissa zipped along on her Rollerblades, while Slobs pulled Sean down the street on his skateboard. Church had been good, and fortunately, the morning had passed without any further disasters. Now the kids were on their way back to Doc's house.

"You think she'll know something more about helping us discover the curse than she did yesterday?" Melissa asked as they headed up the sidewalk toward their friend's front door.

Sean shrugged. "You got any better ideas?"

Melissa shook her head.

"She's always thinking," Sean said. "Maybe she's come up with something."

Doc was in her laboratory—where else?—bent over a sizzling, smoking experiment. A foul-smelling green liquid bubbled up and down in a test tube that she held with tongs over a small burner. In her white smock, with the flame reflecting on her face, Melissa thought she looked a little bit like a mad scientist. In fact, the whole scene reminded her of something she'd seen in an old Frankenstein movie. She half expected Igor to come shuffling out of the darkness with a brain in a jar.

But this was not the movies. It was only Midvale, and nobody had any brains in a jar here—just the greenish liquid in that test tube. She wondered what wonderful benefits that liquid would bring to the world. Could it be a cure for cancer? A formula that would grow crops in the desert? Maybe a new fuel that would cause an ordinary car to travel at the speed of sound. Whatever it was, it had to be amazing. Doc was always inventing something amazing . . . even when those inventions backfired. (Which they usually did!)

Now the woman was removing the test tube from the flame and pouring the liquid into several small bottles to cool. As she did, Sean stepped to the keyboard on her workbench and typed, *What is that stuff, Doc?*

Doc signed something with her hands, but Sean, who

55

was still learning sign language, couldn't quite understand.

What did you say? he asked. *Something about a canoe full of grizzly bears going over Niagara Falls?*

Melissa, who was only a little better at reading sign language, gave him a look. "I think it's something to do with the head or brain," she said.

Doc shook her head, grabbed the keyboard, and typed, *It's a hair restorer.*

"A hair restorer!" Sean exclaimed. Then he signed, *You mean it grows hair?*

I hope so, Doc answered.

Melissa tried to hide her disappointment. A cure for cancer? Yeah, right. So much for Doc's great and noble inventions.

I got the idea when I saw that reporter on TV, Doc typed.

"Cool!" Sean said. "Can this grow hair on anybody?"

It should, Doc typed. *Why?*

"Oh, I don't know," he said. But of course Sean's thoughts had already turned to his face . . . or more precisely, the *lack* of hair on his face.

"You're beautiful, babe!" a high-pitched electronic voice said. "I love ya! Don't change a thing!"

"Jeremiah!" Sean and Melissa both turned and shouted in unison.

There he was in all of his green glory. But instead of

appearing on Doc's monitor, Melissa's video game, or Sean's digital watch, he stood out in the open—like a real person! Though you could also see through him, like he wasn't completely there.

He was still wearing Rafael Ruelas's ridiculous wig and clutching a microphone in his hand. But what was with the pair of sunglasses he wore? And why was he acting like some kind of TV celeb?

He winked at Melissa. "Have your people call my people!"

Before Melissa could respond, he turned to Sean. "Hey, babe. Let's do lunch sometime."

Sean nodded, but he was still too busy eyeing Doc's hair-restoring liquid and daydreaming about how great he'd look with a goatee.

Melissa turned toward Doc. *How did this happen?* she signed.

Doc typed, *That reporter stepped in the puddle and—*

I understand that, Melissa interrupted. *But Jeremiah's never been able to stay out in the real world this long before.*

I think it has to do with the sunspots, Doc typed. *We're passing through a time of tremendous solar activity and—*

Suddenly Jeremiah turned toward Melissa. "You want

an autograph, little lady?" he asked. "I'd be happy to give you one!"

Melissa just stared.

Doc resumed typing. *He seems to be trapped out here until the sunspots pass. That could be another week, maybe more*, she signed.

"Oh no," Misty groaned. *That could get dangerous.*

Doc nodded, but Jeremiah didn't seem to hear. "I'd like to stick around," he said, "but you know how busy we reporters are. Gotta get to the bottom of this curse story."

"Get to the bottom of it?" Melissa asked. "The last thing you told us was you didn't want anything to do with the curse, that you were scared and leaving town."

"Scared?" Jeremiah asked. "You got me mixed up with somebody else, kid. There's no fear in *this* reporter." He stood at attention and saluted. "So, until we meet again, from all of us at Channel 34 News, good night and God bless!" And then . . .

POOF!

. . . he was gone. Just like that. Off to who knows where.

Needless to say, it was quite a shock. But as Melissa turned to Doc to discuss what had happened, it was obvious Sean had something even more important on his mind . . . namely, his looks. Already he had moved closer to the hair-restoration tonic. *It wouldn't hurt anything if I took a couple of drops*, he thought. *What harm could it do?*

While Doc and Melissa remained distracted, he gently picked up the beaker and, ever so carefully, sprinkled just a few drops into his hand and rubbed them onto his chin.

A moment later, Melissa asked, "So, Sean, what do you think?" She started turning toward him. "Is what's happened to Jeremiah somehow related to everything else that's—EEEEEEEK!" She let out the world's scariest scream. In fact, it was so loud that it made Sean's hair stand up.

And believe me, Sean had plenty of hair to stand up! Because, as usual, Doc's invention had even more power than she'd planned. Now there was hair all over Sean's face. And it was still growing. In fact, he was already looking like the Wolfman on a bad hair day!

But of course Sean saw none of this. "What's wrong?" he asked.

"What have you done with Sean?" Melissa screamed at him. "And who are you?"

"What do you mean, who am I?" Sean asked. "It's me!"

Hearing her brother's voice come out of someone who looked like he'd just arrived from the Planet of the Apes was more than Melissa could bear. Without a word she suddenly collapsed into a heap on the floor.

"Sis," Sean raced to her and kneeled at her side. "Sis, what's wrong?"

Slobs, who had been asleep on the floor, was now standing. Her hackles were raised and she was growling. Growling at Sean.

"Slobs," Sean called, "what's wrong? Here, girl, come here." He held his hand out to her. And that's when he got a glimpse of it—his hand was covered with thick, coarse dark hair.

"AAAAGGHHH!" he screamed . . . and a moment later joined his sister, passed out on the floor.

5

My Brother, the Wolfman

SUNDAY, 15:15 PDST

"Who? What . . . where am I?" Sean asked as he sat up.

Then he remembered.

He was on the middle of the floor in Doc's laboratory . . . where he had fainted after realizing he'd turned himself into a creature who looked like a Pokémon card reject. And to top it off, there were now Melissa's kind, soft, understanding words:

"You always have to do something like this, don't you!" she demanded.

"Take it easy, sis," he pleaded. "This situation is hairy enough already." He gave a grin. Nothing like a little humor to lighten things up.

But Melissa was not smiling back. "This isn't the time for your stupid jokes, Sean. Every time Doc invents something, you wind up using it to cause a big mess."

"Okay, I admit it," he smirked. "I did a *hair*brained thing."

Melissa put her hands on her hips. "You are NOT funny!"

"Lighten up, will ya?" Sean said as he admired his hairy reflection in a mirror. "It's no big deal." *I'm sure Doc has an antidote*, he turned and signed to the woman. *Right, Doc?*

Unfortunately, Doc was already shaking her head.

Please, he signed, *tell me you have an antidote!*

She shook her head again and looked at the floor.

Sean took another look in the mirror. "What am I gonna do?" he whined. "I look like that guy from *Star Wars*."

It's true. He was doing a pretty good Chewbacca impression.

In the meantime, Slobs cautiously crept across the floor to sniff Sean's hand. She wasn't sure who this guy was, but he sure sounded like her master.

Melissa let out a long sigh and put a hand on her brother's hairy shoulder. "Well, I do have one idea," she said. "But I'm not sure you're going to like it."

"Anything," he whined as he started to scratch his fur. "This stuff really itches."

Melissa turned toward Doc and signed, *Have you got any shaving cream?*

Several blocks away, KC, Spalding, and Bear (Sean and Melissa's friends—well, sort of friends) pedaled their bikes down Main Street toward Midvale Lake and the Fourteenth Annual Chamber of Commerce Fish-a-Thon. The contest brought one hundred or so of the area's best fishermen together to compete for cash prizes.

Everyone knew KC as the toughest girl in town. Spalding, who was a brain, was the richest. As for their roly-poly pal, Bear . . . well, he wasn't tough, smart, or rich. But he did like to eat. And if KC was going fishing, he'd be sure to stick around to eat whatever she caught!

KC's brand-new rod and reel poked out from the rack on her bike, bouncing up and down as she sped along. Spalding rode beside her. And Bear, as usual, lagged far behind. He could have kept up with them if he wanted, but Bear was never in a hurry about anything!

"So," Spalding called to KC, "are you quite convinced that you will once again capture the prize for being the most proficient angler?"

KC gave him a blank look. "Mind saying that again—in English?!" she asked.

"Do you think you'll catch the most fish again this year?"

KC reached over and patted her new reel. "With this baby and your brains, there's no doubt about it."

Spalding smiled. He didn't care much about fishing, but he enjoyed calculating where the fish would be hiding and what kind of bait would attract them.

"How come you know so much about fish, anyway?" KC asked as they came to a stop and hopped off their bikes near the dock of the lake.

Spalding sighed wearily. "Don't you understand yet? I know absolutely everything about everything!"

KC was about to argue but stopped herself. The reason was simple. He really did seem to know everything about everything.

Up ahead, a couple dozen fishermen stood in a circle, reading a sign posted on the dock's main gate.

"Well, I don't care what it says!" one of them shouted.

"We'd better listen to her if you ask me," someone else said.

"Well, nobody's asking you!"

"What's going on?" KC asked.

"I don't know," Spalding said.

They parked their bikes and pushed their way to the front of the crowd. And there, in crudely written red letters, hung this sign:

WARNING!
I HAVE PLACED A CURSE UPON THESE WATERS!
FISH HERE AT YOUR OWN RISK!

SUNDAY, 16:03 PDST

Ever so carefully, Melissa shaved the last bit of hair off of her brother's chin. She set the razor down on Doc's workbench and stood back to admire her work.

"There," she said. "Your face looks great . . . well, at least normal . . . well, at least for you."

"Ha-ha," Sean said. "Very funny."

"Actually, I did a pretty good job," Melissa said, "even if I do say so myself." She looked down at the hair that covered her brother's arms and hands. "But I have no idea what we're going to do about the rest of you."

She handed her brother a small mirror so he could check out the job she'd done on his face.

Sean smiled at his reflection. "Thanks, sis, that looks . . . OH NO!"

"What's wrong?"

Sean tried to speak, but no words would come. Instead, he watched in silent horror as the hair began to grow back! It sprouted from his chin, his cheeks, even his forehead. And don't even ask about inside his ears and nose.

He looked helplessly over at Doc, who had already started working on an antidote. *Hurry up, Doc*, he signed, then began to scratch again. *Please!*

A moment later Doc was rushing over with a bubbling brown concoction in a beaker. She quickly handed it to Sean and motioned for him to drink it.

Sean took the beaker and gave it a smell. *You gotta be kidding*, he signed. *This stuff smells worse than Melissa's cooking!*

Doc gave no answer but again motioned for him to drink.

What else could he do? So, holding his nose and taking a deep breath, he gulped it down. When he finally finished, he let go a loud . . .

BUURRRP!

This stuff tastes nasty, he signed. Then, holding out his hands, he waited for the hair to disappear.

It didn't.

A full minute passed before Doc shook her head in disappointment. Then she turned and went back to her workbench to recheck her data.

"How about paint remover?" Melissa volunteered. "Maybe that'll get the hair off!"

"I'll try anything," Sean groaned while scratching and looking at his hairy reflection in the mirror. "Just hurry, it's getting worse!"

But little did Sean realize how worse, worse could get. . . .

6

Hook, Line, and a Sinking Feeling!

SUNDAY, 16:07 PDST

The president of the Midvale Chamber of Commerce pulled a handkerchief from his pocket and mopped the perspiration from his forehead. "Maybe we ought to cancel the contest," he said. "At least for this year."

"That's crazy!" KC's gravelly little voice exclaimed. "I'm not afraid of any stupid curse. It's all a bunch of baloney!" She turned to Spalding. "Isn't that right?"

Spalding pushed his glasses up on his nose. "From a scientific perspective, I'd concur that—"

"See! I told you," she interrupted. "So if you guys don't want to fish, please step aside. I've got some big ones to catch."

"The little boy's right," shouted a tall, skinny man with a long, crooked nose.

"Girl!" KC corrected, pulling off her baseball cap so that her hair fell to her shoulders.

"Er, sorry," said the skinny man. "She's right, we can't give in to this thing!"

"I agree!" shouted a woman in a sundress. "Let's fish!"

The crowd cheered as KC stepped to the lakeshore, baited her hook, and cast her line into the water. But something happened on her backswing. Her hook got caught. She yanked hard, but it wouldn't come loose.

"Hey!" someone yelped. "You've got my pants caught with your—"

Too late. KC yanked again and . . .

RIIIIIIIIIP!

. . . she tore the seat right out of the skinny man's trousers, revealing his boxer underwear covered with little red valentine hearts.

"Look out!" It was Bear, finally arriving on his bike. He was heading toward the dock, frantically waving his hands and shouting, "No brakes! I can't stop!"

Half of the group on the dock leaped to the right to get out of the way. The other half leaped to the left. Unfortunately, each leaped the wrong way, which meant they leaped . . .

KER-WHAM!

. . . right into each other. They barely had time to

scramble back to their feet before Bear began mowing them down like bowling pins and sending them . . .

SPLISH! SPLASH! SPLISH!

. . . tumbling into the cold lake!

A moment later, he also . . .

KA-SPLASSH!

. . . joined them, followed right behind by his . . .

SPLOOOOP!

. . . bicycle.

Not far away, two men sat in a rowboat on the lake, dangling their fishing lines into the water. One of them suddenly jumped to his feet.

"I've caught something!" he shouted.

"So have I!" yelled his friend. "And it's huge!"

"So is mine!"

They were both right! It *was* huge. So big, in fact, that it yanked both of them right out of their boat and . . .

K-SPLOOOP!
K-SPLISH!

. . . into the water, still holding their fishing rods.

Suddenly the huge creature they had caught came into sight.

Was it a largemouth bass? Was it a record rainbow trout? No . . . it was . . . it was . . . a . . .

Bear!

The boy came up out of the water, sputtering, gasping for breath, and dragging the two fishermen behind him, their lines wrapped around his arms and legs.

It was obvious that the fishing tournament was *not* getting off to a good start. The president of the Midvale Chamber of Commerce looked around at the minidisasters that had suddenly occurred and clapped his hands. "Attention, please," he shouted. "Attention. This tournament is canceled!"

He didn't see the binoculars that were peeking out from behind an oak tree a hundred yards down the beach.

Nor did he see the mysterious, tall, thin woman behind those binoculars.

But she saw him. Perfectly. She pulled behind the tree, made a few notations in the notebook, and chuckled softly over the comedy of errors she had just witnessed.

"It's working," she whispered. "Even better than I thought."

SUNDAY, 17: 28 PDST

Back in Doc's laboratory, Melissa was panting as if she'd just run ten miles. An assortment of lotions, creams, razors, scissors, hair removers, nail-polish removers, and tweezers lay scattered across Doc's floor. She'd spent every ounce of energy trying to get the hair off of her brother's face, but nothing worked.

She glanced up at Sean, who sat holding his hairy face in his hairy hands and mumbling, "It's the curse, it's the curse, I know it's the curse."

"Don't say that," she scolded. "It's not a curse. It's just . . ."

"What, then?" he asked, looking up at her. "If it's not the curse, then why is this happening to me?"

Melissa shook her head. "I'm not sure, but just because bad stuff happens doesn't mean—"

She was interrupted as Doc approached with yet another antidote. And for the seventh time, Sean took it in his hands, pinched his nose, and swallowed.

And for the seventh time, nothing happened. . . .

"Ooooooooooh!"

Except for the torturing of Sean's taste buds. And the flip-flopping of his stomach. "I don't feel so good," he moaned. He pushed out of his chair and slowly crossed the room to the window. "We can't even go home," he said. "Somebody might see me."

Melissa glanced at her watch. "It'll be dark soon," she said. "We can go home then."

"But what about tomorrow?" Sean asked. He held out his ape-man arms. "I can't go to school looking like this!"

"You'll just have to stay home sick," Melissa said. "I'll ask Spalding to get your homework." She gestured to the workbench, where Doc was busily mixing more chemicals into another test tube. "In the meantime, maybe she'll come up with an antidote."

"I hope so," Sean said as he caught a glimpse of his reflection in the window. "Otherwise they're going to put me in the zoo!"

MONDAY, 15:20 PDST

When Melissa came home from school the next day, she found Sean sitting at the computer in his room, surfing the Internet and, of course, scratching.

Nothing had changed . . . except he was looking less and less like her brother and more and more like Bigfoot.

"I thought you'd never get here," Sean said as Melissa tossed his math and history books on the bed. "Did you go by Doc's?"

Melissa nodded. "Nothing new. She's still working on an antidote."

Sean sighed loudly and resumed scratching.

"What about you?" Melissa asked. "Got any new ideas? Any leads on this so-called curse?"

Sean punched a button to log off his computer. "As a matter of fact, I do," he said. "If we go over to City Hall, we can check old deeds and property records."

"And?" Melissa asked.

"And we can find out who used to own the land where they built the new high school."

Melissa shook her head, not understanding. "How will that help?"

Sean explained, "If we know who used to own the land, then maybe we can figure out who put the curse on Midvale."

"*Supposed* curse," Melissa corrected.

"Yeah, right," Sean said sarcastically as he looked into the mirror. "*Supposed* curse."

Melissa could have said something, but she didn't feel much like arguing.

"Anyway," Sean continued, "finding the past owner will at least give us a place to start."

Melissa nodded. "So, tell me again where I go when I get to City Hall?"

"What do you mean, *I*?" Sean demanded. "I'm going with you."

"Looking like that?!" Melissa scoffed. "I don't think so, big brother."

"I've got it all figured out," Sean said as he rose and disappeared into the bathroom. Moments later he came out wearing one of Dad's old overcoats and the straw hat Mom used to wear when she worked in her flower garden. He had turned up the overcoat's collar to hide his chin and bent the hat's brim down over his face. The finishing touch of this elegant ensemble was one of Mom's old scarves, which he wrapped around his neck, hiding any of the remaining hair.

He twirled in front of his sister, giving his best supermodel impression. "How do I look?" he asked.

"Weird. You look really weird."

"Better to look weird than to be mistaken for an ape."

Melissa had to admit he was right. This way people would think he was strange, but at least they wouldn't go crazy.

"Well, what are we waiting for?" Sean asked. "Let's get going. . . ."

With the hat pulled down over his eyes, Sean couldn't really see where they were going, so Melissa held her brother's elbow as they walked along.

They hadn't gone more than fifty yards down the sidewalk when she whispered, "Uh-oh! Here comes trouble."

"Trouble?"

"Mrs. Tubbs!"

Sean sneaked a peek. Sure enough, Mrs. Tubbs and Precious had chosen this very time for their midafternoon stroll, one of fourteen walks she took that fat cat on every day. Unfortunately, the exercise didn't seem to be doing Precious much good. He still looked like a barrel with feet. A rich, snobby barrel with feet. He wore his rhinestone collar and, as usual, held his head high in the air.

"Why, Melissa Hunter," Mrs. Tubbs gushed, "how are you today, my dear?" She reached over and pinched Melissa's cheek like a little baby's.

Uh-oh, Melissa thought. *She must want something.* That was the only time she ever tried to be nice to the Hunter kids.

Melissa did her best to smile back politely. "I'm just fine, thank you."

"And who is this handsome gentleman you have with you?"

Sean pulled the hat a little bit farther down over his face.

"Oh, uh, this is, this is . . . my grandfather!"

"Your grandfather? Why, didn't I meet him last year at—"

"Er . . . I mean my *great*-grandfather," Melissa interrupted.

"I see." Mrs. Tubbs stood there with a frozen smile stuck on her face. She seemed to be waiting for something. Finally she spoke. "Well, aren't you going to introduce me?" she asked. She cupped her hand to her mouth and whispered, "He seems like a very nice man. And handsome, too!"

"Oh, well, you see, Mrs. Tubbs, he, uh . . . er . . . ah . . . he doesn't speak English."

"He doesn't?"

"No, ma'am, he only speaks, uh . . . Geranium."

Melissa wished she could take the word back as soon as it leaped out of her mouth.

"Geranium?" Mrs. Tubbs exclaimed. "I've never heard of such a thing."

"Oh yes, ma'am. He comes from the country of . . . Gerania. It's where the plant came from."

"Really?"

"Really." Melissa felt pretty bad lying to Mrs. Tubbs, but she didn't know what else to do.

"Well, my dear," Mrs. Tubbs said, "since he's your great-grandfather, I'm sure you must be able to speak a few words of Geranium."

Melissa started to protest, but Mrs. Tubbs cut her off.

"Would you please tell him that I'm very happy to meet him?"

Melissa took a deep breath. She turned toward Sean. "Oh, Grapapapadapa," she began. "Gork snort forken brazen iken sniken caduzeen tubbsy wubbsy."

Sean nodded. "Broinka!"

"What a beautiful language," Mrs. Tubbs exclaimed. "It sounds very much like Italian to me. Now, would you please tell him that I'd like to invite him over for dinner. How about tomorrow night?"

"Tubbsy wubbsy orken shadorken glimisen Frere Jacques, dormez-vous?" Melissa was feeling pretty comfortable with this language she'd just invented. And she was getting more and more used to not telling Mrs. Tubbs the truth. Maybe lying wasn't as bad as everyone always said. Just as long as you don't get caught at it.

Again Sean nodded. "Broinka, broinka!"

"Is that all he can say?" Mrs. Tubbs asked. " 'Broinka, broinka'?"

"Oh, he's a little shy." It was another lie, but hey, the first one worked, so why not keep it up? And this lie would have worked, as well, except at that exact moment, a sudden gust of wind lifted Sean's hat completely off his head!

"EEEEEEE!" Mrs. Tubbs screamed. "He's not shy! He's a . . . a . . . gorilla!"

The jig was up! And so was Melissa's career in lying.

79

7

Superstar Jeremiah to the Rescue

MONDAY, 16:13 PDST

"Please, Mrs. Tubbs," Melissa pleaded. "Let me explain."

But the woman was too scared to listen. Come to think of it, she was too scared to run, as well. All she could do was scream.

"AUGHHHH . . ."

Lots and lots of screaming.

But not Precious. Despite his weight problem, it only took a grand total of 1.9 seconds for him to make his way thirty feet up into the nearest elm tree.

And still Mrs. Tubbs continued screaming. "AUGHHH! A gorilla! A gorilla! Help! Help!"

Now it was Sean's turn to try to reason with her. "Listen, Mrs. Tubbs, it's me. It's Se—"

But that's all he got out before . . .

"OHHhhh . . ."

Mrs. Tubbs' legs crumpled and . . .

KA-THWACK!

. . . she hit the pavement. Apparently a talking gorilla was more than she could handle.

Sean kneeled at her side. "Mrs. Tubbs . . . Mrs. Tubbs . . . Can you hear me? Mrs. Tubbs, wake up."

But Mrs. Tubbs was in no mood to wake up. Instead, she suddenly started to . . .

ZZZNNNNNXXXX!

. . . snore.

"She's fainted," Melissa explained.

Sean looked up. "Really? I just thought it was time for her afternoon nap."

Melissa ignored the sarcasm. "What are we going to do?" she asked.

"Maybe we could carry her home and put her on her couch," Sean suggested.

"What good would that do?"

"Then when she wakes up, she'll just think she's been dreaming!"

Melissa looked down at the woman skeptically. "I don't know, Sean, she's awfully big. Do you really think we can carry her?"

He shrugged. "Won't know unless we try."

Melissa stooped down and slipped her arms under Mrs. Tubbs' arms. "Grab her feet and let's see what we can do."

"Right," Sean nodded. He slipped out of the heavy coat and gave her a hand. Meanwhile, high overhead, Precious watched the proceedings with a rather bored expression on his face. A more heroic animal might have charged to his master's rescue. But Precious had more important things on his mind, like wondering if that gorilla was going to eat the old woman, then who was going to feed her cat.

Unfortunately, with such important thoughts on his mind, the big cat didn't notice that the branch that was holding him had begun to crack under his weight.

Sean groaned as he lifted Mrs. Tubbs' legs. "This woman is heavy!"

"Told you," Melissa said, doing her best to hold up her end, until suddenly—

KE-RACK!

. . . the elm tree branch gave way!

Precious let out a yowl, "MEOWWRRR!" (which is cat-talk for either "Look out below!" or "Is somebody down there going to catch me?").

Whichever it was, Sean looked up just in time to see

the cat's huge body heading toward him like a fur-covered meteor from outer space until . . .

K-THUNK!

. . . Precious landed on top of his head and dug in his claws!

"Aaaagggh!" Sean screamed as he dropped Mrs. Tubbs' legs and whirled about trying to pull the cat off of his head.

Believe it or not, that was the good news. Unfortunately, it got a little worse. Because at that very moment, the fifty-member Midvale Seniors Bicycle Club came riding by. Immediately the brakes on all fifty ten-speed bikes . . .

SCREEETCH!

. . . were hit, and they all came to a stop!

"Look at that!" shouted the club's president. "It's a gorilla!"

"Look at the way it's dressed," another observed. "Must have escaped from the circus."

"It's trying to kill the old woman!" an older man shouted.

"Look how that cat's fighting him off!" another added.

By now Sean and Precious had managed to stagger into the middle of the street—the cat hanging on tight, Sean trying to pry him loose.

"That cat's a hero!" someone yelled.

"Come on!" the president shouted. "We've got to help!"

"But that's a gorilla you're talking about!"

"There's only one of him, and there's fifty of us!" the president yelled. "Come on, let's go!"

It was just about then that Sean finally managed to pry the big cat off his face. Precious hit the ground running for parts unknown. But Sean, although he'd escaped the frying pan, was now heading straight into the fire. He stood facing fifty angry senior citizen bicyclists, who began descending upon him like so many . . . well, angry senior citizen bicyclists.

"Get him! Grab him! Don't let him get away!"

"Run, Sean!" Melissa screamed. "Run!"

Sean didn't have to be told twice. He headed down the street, running for all he was worth.

"AFTER HIM!"

He'd only traveled fifty yards before he saw a kid with a skateboard. Now, as best he figured, Sean had three options:

OPTION ONE: Ask the kid nicely if he could borrow the skateboard and promise that he would return it (while hoping the child would actually trust a talking gorilla).

OPTION TWO: Try to explain the situation (which

would be almost as difficult as getting him to trust a talking gorilla).

OPTION THREE: Scare the kid off the board, grab it, and skate like the wind.

After carefully examining his choices, Sean decided upon:

"GROWLLLLL!"

Option Three.

The kid screamed, lost his balance, and fell off. Sean hopped on and took off, the senior citizens right behind him.

"Look at the way he skates!" one of them shouted. "He must be trained."

Sean would have liked to stick around and explain the situation, but with fifty bicyclists racing after him, he figured now was probably not the best time. Instead, he bore down, skating as fast as he could.

Unfortunately, the senior citizens bore down, too, pedaling as fast as they could.

Sean turned onto Second Avenue and looked over his shoulder. The bicyclists were right behind him. Suddenly he heard . . .

HOOONKKK!

He spun around just in time to see . . .

HOOONKKK! HOOONKKK!!

... a giant soft drink truck coming right at him!

The big truck swerved hard to the left. The good news was that it missed Sean. The bad news was that a dozen crates of soda slid off the truck and ...

BLAM—*Fizzzzzz* ...
BLAM—*Fizzzzzz* ...
BLAM—*Fizzzzzz* ...

... hit the pavement, exploding and spraying soda in all directions.

Pedestrians ran for cover ... but those bicyclists just kept on coming.

Sean swerved to the left, right in front of another ...

HOOONKKK!

... truck. This one was carrying produce to Ramsey's Market. The driver stomped on his brakes, which caused the entire truck to slide to a sideways stop, sending an avalanche of cantaloupes ...

K-PLOP ... K-PLOP ... K-PLOP ...

... cascading into the street, where they began to ...

ROLL ... ROLL ... ROLL ... ROLL ...

... down the street like bowling balls.

And still the bicyclists pursued him.

Sean turned sharply again, zipping into a narrow alley that ran between a hardware store and a coffee shop. Not a bad choice, except for the fact that the alley was a dead end with no way out! He skidded to a stop and frantically looked for a way of escape.

Several of the stores' back doors faced the alley.

Please, God! he prayed, racing toward them. *Help me!*

He grabbed the nearest door and tried to turn the knob.

It wouldn't budge.

He tried the next.

Different door, same problem. Each one seemed to be tightly locked.

Meanwhile, the bicyclists (and a few angry truck drivers) rounded the corner. "There he is!" they shouted. "He's not getting away now!"

Sean turned toward them, his back against the wall, as they continued to close in. *Please, God. Please . . .*

8

If This Isn't a Curse, I Don't Know What Is!

MONDAY, 16:48 PDST

Sean looked left and then right, still praying under his breath that God would help him escape. He definitely needed a miracle to get him out of this one.

The mob slowed to a stop ten or fifteen feet away. It was obvious they were unsure what to do next.

Finally one of the truck drivers stepped forward. He was a strong guy with a red face. A red *angry-looking* face. He reached into his pants pocket for something.

Sean's heart stopped. What was it? A knife? A gun?

And then he pulled out . . . a handkerchief. He began mopping his forehead. "Shucks," he said. "It's kind of hard to be mad at the little feller, what with him bein' so cute and all."

"Cute?" one of the old ladies from the bicycle group

scorned. "I wouldn't be surprised if he had something to do with the curse that has this town in such a—" She stopped midsentence. "Well, now that you mention it, he is kind of a cute monkey."

Sean didn't know which was worse. To die at the hands of an angry mob or to be considered a "cute monkey." Fortunately, he didn't have to make a decision because, off to the left, a door suddenly opened. A woman stepped out into the alley, saw the group, and quickly scurried past them.

Sean watched, sensing something strangely familiar about the lady. And then he saw it!

The spidery tattoo on the back of her neck!

Sean pointed. He sputtered. He wanted to tell everyone who the woman was, but the words wouldn't come.

"Well!" the truck driver finally said as he pulled a cell phone out of his other pocket. "I guess I oughta call Midvale Animal Control."

"Maybe they'll shoot him with one of them tranquilizer guns," one of the senior citizens said. "Keep him in the zoo till his owner is found."

If Sean was nervous before, he was definitely in a panic now. He looked back to the driver, who was frowning at his phone.

"What's wrong?" the head biker asked.

"I don't know. I can't get anything but static. What in

the world's wrong with this thing?"

Static? Sean thought. *Must be those sunspots again. They just keep on—*

But his thoughts were interrupted by a humming noise that filled the air. It was quickly followed by a loud . . .

POP!

. . . and suddenly Jeremiah was standing next to him—his red eyes glowing and his green skin shining. He still held a microphone and he was still wearing Rafael's goofy-looking wig.

"*Earwitness News!*" he shouted.

The crowd gasped.

He stepped toward the truck driver, thrusting the microphone into his face. "We've received reports that a killer gorilla is on the loose in the area. Tell us, sir. Have you seen anything like that?"

The big man would have answered, but he was too busy spinning around, taking off running, and screaming for his life.

And he wasn't the only one screaming. After one look at Jeremiah's glowing green face, the rest of the mob turned and ran like scared rabbits. "Monster!" they screamed. "Let me out of here! It's more of the curse!"

Not understanding, Jeremiah ran down the alley after them. "What about you, sir?" he shouted. "Have you seen anything?"

"AUGHHH . . ."

"How about you, ma'am?"

"AUGHHH . . ."

And suddenly, before he knew it, Sean was all alone in the alley. Taking a deep breath, he lifted his eyes to heaven. "Thank you, God," he said. "I don't know how you did it, but thank you."

"Sean! Sean, are you okay?"

He looked over to see Melissa running down the alley toward him.

"Woof! Woof!"

And Slobs, too . . . though it was obvious the dog didn't know whether to attack the hairy monster or jump up and lick his master's face.

"I thought they were going to kill you," Melissa said as she arrived, catching her breath. "How did you get away?"

"A miracle," Sean answered.

"A miracle?"

"I'll explain later," Sean said. "But the important thing is that I saw her."

"Saw her? Her who?"

"The curse lady. She came through that door right over there." He raced to it and tried to open it.

No luck.

"I wonder what she was doing in there," he said.

"Do you know what building it is?" Melissa asked.

He shook his head.

"Let's go around to Third Avenue and find out."

"Aren't you forgetting something?" Sean asked. He held out his arms. "How am I going to go into the streets looking like this? Come to think of it, how am I going to go *anywhere* looking like this?"

"I already thought of that," Melissa said. "That's why I swung by Smiley's Pet Shop and bought this." She reached into her backpack and pulled out . . .

"A collar?" Sean frowned. "And a leash? What am I supposed to do with these?"

"Put them on," Melissa answered.

"Put them on?" Sean scowled at her. "Are you crazy? Why would I want to do that?"

"So people will think you're my pet monkey!"

"Monkey?!" Sean looked at her like she had a screw loose.

"Or gorilla, or whatever. You see, if people think you're my pet, they'll leave you alone."

"Your . . ." Sean could barely get out the word, "*pet?!*"

"That's right," Melissa grinned.

"No way," Sean said. "I'm not wearing this collar or this leash. Never!"

Melissa shrugged. "Have it your way. But if you've got a better idea, you'd better tell me before the police get here."

"Police," Sean scoffed. "What police?"

"Those police," Melissa said, motioning to the patrol car just pulling into the alley.

Sean spun around and saw it. "Oh no!" he cried. "We've got to do something! Help me think of something!"

In response, Melissa simply held out the collar and leash.

He looked at them. Then at her. Then back to them again. "All right!" he finally growled. "Give them to me!" He slipped the collar over his head and attached the leash.

"You've got to be more convincing than that," Melissa whispered. "Do something."

"Like what?"

"I don't know—make monkey noises or something."

Sean gave her a look.

She gave it back at him.

A sickening feeling filled his stomach. She had a point. It might take more than just a leash and a collar to convince them. Reluctantly, and with more than a little grumbling, Sean stooped over and began talking like a monkey. "Oooh-oooh, eeee-eeee, aaah-aaah!"

The police car had rolled to a stop and the officer called from his window, "Little girl, you shouldn't be back here in this alley. We just got a report that there's some kind of wild animal loose in the area."

"Wild animal?" Melissa tried to sound frightened. "Really?"

The policeman nodded. "You haven't seen anything strange, have you?"

"Oh no, sir," she said, sweetly. "Not a thing."

"Well, you be careful," the officer said. He put his car into reverse. "Oh, and one other thing."

"Yes, officer?"

"That monkey of yours is really cute. How long have you had him?"

"As long as I can remember," Melissa answered.

"Does he do any tricks?"

"Does he do tricks?" Melissa answered. "Watch this." She turned to her brother. "Come on, Seanny Boy," she said, trying to hide her smile. "Show the nice man how you can stand on your head."

If looks could kill, Melissa would be dead.

But she knew she had her brother right where she wanted him. Considering all the mean things he'd ever done to her, this was definitely payback time. "Come on, Seanny," she coaxed. "Come on. Show the nice man how you can stand on your head."

With no alternative but to obey, Sean reluctantly knelt down, put his head on the hard pavement, and slowly stood on his head.

"Excellent." The policeman applauded. "Nice work.

How about cartwheels? Can he turn cartwheels?"

"Cartwheels are his specialty!" Melissa exclaimed. "Just watch!"

She clapped her hands. "Come on, boy, do a cartwheel. Do a cartwheel, Seanny Boy. Come on."

Once again, Sean obeyed. But not before whispering, "I'll get you for this."

Melissa could only laugh. She was having the time of her life.

MONDAY, 17:07 PDST

"How could you humiliate me like that?" Sean pouted as he scratched.

"Oh, come on. It was fun," Melissa said. Then, unable to resist, she added, "You cute little monkey, you."

Sean did his best to ignore her as they walked along Third Avenue, looking for the building that the mysterious "curse lady" had exited. Unfortunately, the humiliation wasn't entirely over, because as he and his sister walked down the street, they heard dozens of comments like:

"What a cute monkey!"

"Where'd you buy him?"

"Does he bite?"

And worst of all: "Is he potty-trained?"

At last they stopped in front of a red brick building.

"Is this it?" Melissa asked.

"I think so," Sean said. "If you went through this building, I think you'd come out . . . yeah . . . right about where that door opens into the alley."

Melissa read the sign on the door. *Jane Williams, Psychologist.* She turned to Sean. "So you think maybe our curse lady is one of her patients?"

Before Sean could answer, a familiar voice rang out behind them. "Hey, I didn't know you had a monkey!"

Sean turned and let out a groan. And for good reason. It was KC, Spalding, and Bear.

"Oh, hi, KC," Melissa answered cheerfully. "He's not really my monkey. I'm just . . . er . . . monkey-sitting for a friend."

KC nodded as Spalding took a step closer and peered into Sean's face. "Boy! I've seen some ugly-looking monkeys before," he said. "But this one takes the cake. Doesn't look like he has a brain in his head."

"You're probably right," Melissa agreed. "But he really is cute."

Cute . . . there was that word again.

KC shrugged. "Whatever."

"You know," Spalding continued, "this creature

appears extremely familiar to me. I feel as if I know him from somewhere."

Melissa tried to change the subject by pointing to the cast on KC's arm. "What happened?"

"You heard about the fishing tournament?" KC asked.

"I heard it was canceled," Melissa said.

"Because it was cursed," KC explained.

Melissa shook her head. "I really don't think there's any such thing as a curse. People just think bad things are going to happen to them, so they do."

"Oh yeah," KC challenged. "Well, maybe you just don't—"

BRRRP! BRRRP!

Melissa reached for her cell phone and answered, "Bloodhounds, Incorporated." She listened for a moment, then answered, "Uh-huh . . . I see . . . uh-huh. We'll be right over!" With that, she hung up and quickly reached for Sean's leash. "I'd love to talk, guys, but we've got an emergency."

"What type of emergency?" KC asked.

But Melissa was already moving along. "It's a secret. Company business." Then, turning to Sean, she called, "Come on, boy, come on!"

Of course, Sean wanted to stay and check out the psychologist's office, but he could tell by the tone of

Melissa's voice that something was up. Besides, he was grateful to get away from KC, Spalding, and Bear.

Melissa gave a tug on his leash. Knowing he still had to play the part, Sean obeyed, took a deep breath, and reluctantly answered, "Oooh—oooh, eeee-eeee, aaah-aaah . . ."

MONDAY, 17:54 PDST

The call was from Doc—or at least from the computer that translated her typing into words. Now Sean sat in her laboratory, staring nervously at the little green pill in his hand. The little green pill that was supposed to be the antidote.

"Go ahead," Melissa urged him. "What are you waiting for?"

Trying his best to appear brave and macho, Sean took a nervous swallow, opened his mouth, and tossed the little pill inside.

Well, at least that's what he tried to do. But instead of tossing it inside, the pill hit one of Sean's front teeth, bounced out of his mouth, and fell to the floor.

"Oops," Sean grinned sheepishly.

Sean, Doc, and Melissa stooped down to look for it.

Unfortunately, Slobs got to it first and . . .

GULLLLLP!

. . . swallowed it.

Melissa stepped back in horror, expecting something terrible to happen to her beloved bloodhound. Instead, all she heard was a very loud . . .

BURRRRP!

Was that it? Was that all? Nothing but a burp?

Apparently so. The big dog just licked her lips and whined as if she wanted another pill. But there was only one more, and Sean wasn't taking any chances with it. He placed it carefully in his mouth, grabbed a glass of water, and swallowed.

Almost instantaneously the gorilla hair began to disappear. Within two minutes it had all fallen off.

"I'm back!" Sean shouted. "Thank you, Doc!" He danced around the room in delight. "Thank you, thank you, thank—"

BRRRP! BRRRP!

Sean stopped dancing long enough to grab the phone by the third ring. "Bloodhounds, Incorporated."

"Sean?"

"Herbie, is that you?"

"Come to the radio station right away," the engineer

cried. "Something terrible has happened!"

MONDAY, 18:08 PDST

At the radio station, Sean and Melissa found their father sitting in a chair behind his desk, his skin black with soot. Tufts of smoke were still rising from his hair, and his clothes were tattered and torn.

"Dad?" Melissa cried. "Dad, are you all right?" She ran to him and threw her arms around him. He hugged her weakly in return.

Sean turned to Herbie. "What happened? He looks like he's been in an explosion."

"He has," Herbie answered.

"I'm okay," Mr. Hunter said. "Just shook up. We went out to make some minor adjustments to the transmitter and—"

Herbie interrupted. "And when I touched the red wire to the green wire, ka-blooey! Right in your dad's face."

"You did what?" Sean asked in disbelief.

"I didn't mean to," Herbie whined. "But you know how this whole town is cursed."

Dad shook his head. "Herbie, there's no curse. If you hadn't been so worried about it in the first place, you would have been paying more attention to what you were doing."

"No way," Herbie argued. "That curse has caused all of us in town a lot of trouble."

The kids seldom saw Dad lose his temper, but he was definitely getting close to it now. "How many times do I have to tell you," he practically shouted, "there's no such thing as a curse!" To make his point, he pounded his fist on his desk.

K-BAM!

His point might have been made better if the desk had not suddenly . . .

K-RUMPLE, K-RUMPLE, K-RUMPLE!

. . . collapsed onto the floor in a heap.

9

Talk About a Close Shave!

MONDAY, 18:19 PDST

"Dad! Are you okay?"

He stood up, swiping the dust off his pants with his hands. "Yeah," he said. "I'm fine. And I still don't believe there's any such thing as a—"

KA-CHOOO!

Suddenly Slobs let loose with the loudest sneeze Melissa had ever heard. Actually, the second loudest sneeze. The loudest was coming up just about . . .

KA-CHOOOOOOOO!

. . . now.

"Sean!" Melissa gasped. "Look!"

"Oh no!" Sean groaned. And for good reason. There on the floor lay a huge pile of doggy hair. Beside it stood

Slobs, completely naked. In fact, she looked like a big pink pig.

"Looks like the antidote takes a little longer to work on dogs," Melissa said.

"Let's hope that's not the only difference," Sean said.

"What do you mean?"

"I mean, I don't want to wind up looking like a . . . ah . . . ah. . . ." he started to sneeze until he stuck his finger under his nose.

"Like what?" Melissa asked.

"Like . . . a . . . ah . . ."

AH-CHOOOOO!

As Sean sneezed, a huge clump of hair fell to the floor. He looked down at it and began to panic. He quickly put his hand to the back of his head, and when he pulled it away, to his horror, he had pulled out an even bigger clump.

"Oh no!" he shouted. "I'm going bald!"

"Don't panic!" Melissa cried.

"What am I gonna do?"

"I don't know. We've gotta get to Doc's! We've got to get to her fast!"

MONDAY 18:52 PDST

By the time the kids arrived at Doc's house, Slobs wasn't the only one bald. Doc quickly ushered Sean to a chair and brought him a smoky, smelly beaker to drink.

"Oh no," Sean groaned. "What is it?"

Doc motioned for him to hurry and drink it.

Reluctantly, Sean held his nose, tilted back his head, and drank. Almost immediately hair began to sprout. That was the good news. Unfortunately, there was some bad. The hair was bright purple. And it wouldn't stop growing. Well, not until it touched the floor . . . which took a grand total of about 23.4 seconds.

"Oh no . . ."

Immediately Doc brought him another beaker. Same smell, same nose holding, and drinking. This time the purple hair completely fell out.

Good.

But now he was the not-so-proud owner of a long white beard.

Not so good.

Doc arrived with another "antidote." Moments later Sean was sporting a green Mohawk.

Then another "antidote." This time a Fu Manchu mustache.

Another and he was bald again.

"You know," Sean said, studying his reflection in the mirror, "bald isn't so bad. I could get used to this."

But Doc wouldn't quit. Not yet. She handed him one final beaker full of a clear, bubbling liquid.

"I don't know," Sean said, holding his stomach. "I'm getting pretty . . .

BURP!

. . . full."

But Doc, who never gives up, insisted he try one more time.

"All right," Sean sighed. "But this is the last." He took the beaker into his hands and everyone watched . . . Melissa, Doc, even Slobs. After taking a deep breath, he tilted back his head and drank one final time.

But nothing happened. Nothing at all.

Once again, Sean sighed. "Well, at least you tried, Doc. And like I said, bald isn't so bad. Maybe I'll just—" And then suddenly . . .

POOF!

. . . Sean was back to normal.

"All right!" he cried. "Way to go!" He reached down and fed the remainder to Slobs and . . .

POOF!

. . . she was back to normal, too!

106

"Great!" Melissa exclaimed. "Now we can get back to the real problem."

"Real problem?" Sean asked, checking his hair in the mirror and making sure it was perfectly combed. "What's more important than my looks?"

"The case," Melissa sighed. "Remember, we were hired to solve a case!"

TUESDAY, 14:49 PDST

Other than Sean's looks, there was one other thing more important than the case. . . .

School.

But the next day, as soon as they were out of class, Melissa and Sean started for the psychologist's office downtown. They'd only traveled a few blocks when Melissa slowed. "What's that sound?" she asked.

Sean shook his head. "I don't hear any—"

"It's real low and rumbly. Don't you hear it?"

"Yeah, now I do. Sounds like a bunch of trucks."

"And it's coming from over there." Melissa pointed toward the new high school.

"Come on," Sean said. "Let's go!"

The closer they got to the school, the louder the noise

grew. What had started as a faint rumble had turned into a deafening roar.

"Look!" Sean said, pointing toward the high school. "Bulldozers!"

Melissa followed his gaze and, sure enough, a half dozen of the huge machines were rolling into the parking lot beside the new high school football field. A man wearing a hard hat and an orange vest was directing them.

Sean and Melissa raced up to him, and Sean tried to shout over the deafening noise. "What's going on?"

The man jerked his thumb at the football field. "We're tearing this field down," he shouted. He cast an eye across the field at the new science building. "And if that doesn't get rid of the curse, then the whole school may have to go."

"You can't do that!" Sean shouted.

"Yeah? Why not?"

Melissa chimed in, " 'Cause there's no such thing as a curse!"

The last of the bulldozers had lined up with the others and, on the man's signal, cut its engine.

"Sure, kid," the big man laughed. "Half the town is crazy with fear . . . and you tell me there's no such thing as a curse."

Sean and Melissa exchanged glances.

The man continued, "Well, curse or no curse, I've got

my orders. At 4:30 sharp, this football field comes down."

Melissa looked at her watch. "That's in ninety minutes!"

He shook his head. "Eighty-seven minutes, to be exact."

"Can't you give us some more time?" Sean asked.

"Give *you* time?" the man frowned. "Why should I give *you* time? Who are you?"

"We're Bloodhounds, Incorporated," Melissa explained, "and we're—"

"Never heard of you," the man said. "Now you kids run along. We've got a job to do." With that, he turned and headed toward the big machines.

"What are we gonna do now?" Melissa cried.

"I'm thinking," her brother answered. "I'm thinking!"

"Well, hurry up!"

"You can't rush genius—give me a second."

In frustration, Melissa turned and started off.

"Hey, where you going?" Sean cried.

"While you're thinking, I'm going to that psychologist's office!"

"Wait a minute," Sean snapped his fingers. "I've got it!"

"What?" Melissa asked.

"Let's go to the psychologist's office."

Melissa slowed to a stop and looked at him.

"Well, don't just stand there," Sean said as he raced past her. "Let's get going!"

Melissa could only stare after her brother, marveling at his intelligence . . . or lack of it.

TUESDAY, 15:11 PDST

"You don't understand," Sean said. "I've got to see the doctor right now. It's an emergency!"

The receptionist pulled her tortoiseshell glasses down her nose and looked over them. "An emergency?" she asked. "Dr. Williams is a psychologist. She can't be bothered with your tummy aches or whatever your problem is."

"It's nothing like that," Sean said. "I *really* need to see her. It's hard to explain."

"I'll bet it is." The woman shook her head and popped her gum. "The doctor is busy."

"Please!" Sean gave her his best puppy dog look. The helpless, pathetic one. The one that always worked on Mom when she was alive. "It's really important!" he pleaded, almost whimpering. "Just ask her. Pleasssse . . ."

The woman looked at him, gave a heavy sigh of frustration, and finally rose to her feet. "Well, all right. I'll ask, but don't expect her answer to be any different from mine."

Sean broke into a grin and whispered to Melissa, "The ol' puppy dog imitation gets them every—"

But when he turned to his sister, she wasn't there. "Misty." He glanced around the office. "Misty, where are you?"

Suddenly the receptionist returned. "Go on in," she answered heavily. "But be quick. Dr. Williams is a very busy woman."

"Thanks," Sean said. He wanted to find his sister, but this was too important an opportunity to pass up. Besides, she'd be fine. Who knows, maybe she'd found another clue outside the building and went to investigate.

In any case, Sean headed past the receptionist and entered the small office. It was filled with about a million books. And not far away, seated behind a large cheery desk, sat Dr. Williams. She was a middle-aged woman, dark-haired and a little skinny. At the moment, she was hunched over a legal pad, writing. When she spoke she didn't even bother looking up. "Yes?"

Sean cleared his throat. "I . . . uh . . . I just wanted to see if I could get some information about one of your patients."

"Sorry," she said, still writing. "I can't tell you that sort of thing. It's confidential."

There was something strangely familiar about the voice, but Sean couldn't place it. Although he was nervous, he wasn't about to give up, not that easily. "Well," he said, "can you tell me if any of your patients use your back door?"

"That's a ridiculous question," she said. "Why would you ask me something like that?"

Sean was getting nowhere fast. But that voice, if he could just place that voice . . .

Meanwhile, Melissa, who had slipped out the front door, had gone around to the alley to try the back door again. This time, to her surprise, it was unlocked. Ever so carefully, she pushed it open. Just a crack.

"Hello!" she called. "Anybody in here?"

No answer. She hesitated for a moment. Should she or shouldn't she? After all, sneaking into back alley doors was not her idea of a good time . . . much less good behavior. Still, the fate of the football field, perhaps the entire town of Midvale, was at stake. So finally, cautiously, she opened the door and entered. It was dark and filled with boxes and stacks of books.

At first she couldn't see. But as her eyes grew accustomed to the darkness, she spotted a long white robe hanging on a hook in the corner. It looked familiar, but she couldn't quite place it. She started toward it, then spotted a notebook lying open on an old desk.

She reached for it and picked it up. Although it was difficult to see in the dim light, she was finally able to begin reading the handwritten pages. A moment later she gasped. "Oh no . . ." And two moments later she half whispered, "Now I understand. . . ."

But she was so engrossed in reading that she didn't see the shadowy figure approach from behind. She may not have seen it, but she heard and felt it when it grabbed her, wrapped a hand over her mouth, and growled, "Gotcha!"

10

Wrapping Up

WHAPPP!

The office door flew open and hit Sean in the back, sending him sprawling forward onto Dr. Williams' desk.

"Oh, sorry, kid," a gruff voice said.

Sean looked up into the face of a giant. A giant with red hair, green eyes, and a kind-looking face. A giant that had a patch across his overalls that read *Carl's Janitorial Service*. A giant who carried Melissa as she kicked and squirmed, trying to get free.

"Sorry to bother ya, Dr. Williams . . . but I found this kid snoopin' around in the back."

Now, ordinarily Sean would have fought to free his sister, but the big man was already setting her down. Besides, Sean was too busy rubbing his chest where he'd hit the doctor's desk. Something in his shirt pocket had really jabbed into him. What in the world. . . ? He reached into his pocket and pulled out the tiny bottle of Doc's hair restoration formula.

I should have gotten rid of this a long time ago, he thought as he momentarily set the bottle on the doctor's in basket so he could rub his chest.

Now that Melissa was free and on her feet, she shouted at the psychologist, "I know who you are! You're the woman who put the curse on Midvale."

Dr. Williams gave a nervous laugh. "What a silly child. Why would I do a thing like that?"

"You wrote about it in your notebook," Melissa answered.

The big giant turned toward the psychologist. "Izzat true, Dr. Williams?"

"Of course not!" she snorted. "She's just trying to save her skin from trespassing. You can go now, Carl. I can handle it from here."

"Yes, ma'am." He turned to Sean. "Sorry 'bout hittin' ya with that door."

Sean gave a nervous nod as the big man turned and strode out of the room, whistling as he went.

The door had barely shut before Dr. Williams picked up her phone.

"What are you doing?" Melissa asked.

"I'm calling the police. I'm sure they have appropriate

penalties for obnoxious kids breaking and entering."

"I think that would be a great idea," Melissa said.

"Misty?!" Sean protested.

"No, that will be great," she insisted. "So when the police come, we can tell them all about the notebook and they can read it for themselves."

Dr. Williams hesitated. "Not if I destroy it."

"You're going to destroy all that work?" Melissa asked. "All that research? I don't think so."

"Research?" Sean asked. "What research?"

"There's never been a curse," Melissa explained. "She's writing a book on the power of the human mind. And she's been using all of us as her guinea pigs."

"You're kidding," Sean said, looking first to the doctor, then to Melissa.

"She wanted to prove that when people believe in bad things—like curses—bad things happen to them."

Suddenly for Sean, it all started to make sense.

"She wanted to prove that if we believe in them, we actually bring the bad things upon ourselves. . . ."

As Melissa spoke, another thought came to Sean's mind. Carefully, he inched his way closer to Dr. Williams.

"She wanted to prove that if people believe in curses, then—"

Suddenly he reached down and pulled the hair away from Dr. Williams' neck.

"What are you doing?" the woman cried. "Get your hands off—"

"It's not a tattoo!" Sean exclaimed. "It's a birthmark! The same birthmark I saw on your neck the night at the football game. And then again when I saw you in the alley! You're the one who—"

"And I was going to get away with it, too, until you brats interfered," Dr. Williams growled. "But my studies will continue." She rose to her feet. "Do you hear me? Neither you nor anyone else is going to stop me! Do you hear me? NO ONE IS GOING TO STOP ME!" Angrily, she pounded her fist on her desk. Well, actually, she missed the desk and caught the corner of her in basket. It flipped up, sending papers and assorted items high into the air.

Including the little bottle of hair restorer.

Sean was the first to spot it heading toward the ceiling. "Look out!" he cried.

Melissa saw it next. Both of them ducked and covered their heads as the little bottle . . .

BOINK!

. . . smashed into the ceiling with just enough force to . . .

KERRACK!

. . . cause it to break open.

Dr. Williams looked up. "What in the world. . . ?" as

the contents of the little bottle rained down over her face and body.

"Ugh!" she cried. "What is that? It smells awful."

But she had no idea what "awful" was . . . until suddenly thick black hair began sprouting from her face, her arms, and her hands.

"Ahhhh!" she cried. Sean and Melissa watched as she frantically fumbled for the small mirror she kept in her top drawer. "What's happening to me?" Seeing herself in the mirror, she let out another scream, worse than the first. "I'm turning into some sort of ape! What's happening? What is that stuff? What's it doing to me?!"

"It's a hair restorer," Sean said casually.

"Well, make it stop, make it stop!"

"There's only one way to stop it," Sean continued.

"How? Tell me how!"

"With the antidote," Melissa said.

"Then get it! Get it!"

"Not so fast," Sean said. "There's something we need you to do first."

"Anything!" she cried. "Anything. Just get me that antidote!!"

119

TUESDAY, 16:23 PDST

Melissa looked at her watch. "Seven minutes to go," she said. "We'll never get to the high school in time!"

"And what if they don't believe me?" Dr. Williams whined.

Melissa looked over at the hairy creature driving them to the school in her Volvo.

"A talking ape?" Sean laughed. "I'm pretty sure they'll believe you."

"Listen!" Melissa cried.

In the distance, the bulldozer engines had come to life.

"I hear them, too!" Sean said.

The destruction had begun!

"We've got to go faster!" Sean shouted.

"They're not supposed to start for five more minutes!" Melissa cried.

Dr. Williams rounded the corner, and the football field came into view. One bulldozer was already heading for a goal post. Her car roared into the parking lot and screeched to a stop. Sean jumped out and frantically waved his arms at the workers. "Stop!" he shouted. "Stop!"

Nobody paid attention—until first one, than another got a look at Dr. Williams. Soon they were all hopping off their machines and running over. After all, it's not every day you get to see an ape-woman drive a car!

As they pushed and gathered around, one of them asked, "What is it?"

"It's Bigfoot," someone ventured.

"More like a Mrs. Bigfoot," another added.

"I'm *not* Bigfoot," Dr. Williams sobbed. "I'm a psychologist!"

"A psychologist!" Everyone shouted the word at the same time.

"There's no telling what they can train animals to do," another exclaimed.

"No," she cried, tears streaming down her hairy face, "I'm a real psychologist. And I'm responsible for the curse. Well, really, there is no curse. You see, I just wanted to win the Nobel Prize and . . ."

"Somebody better call the mayor," a worker shouted.

"The *mayor*?" another cried. "Better make that the TV station!"

"Oh no," Dr. Williams sobbed. "I can't go on TV, not like this." She turned to Sean. "Please, please, I've got to have that antidote."

"After that we'll go straight to City Hall and explain?" Sean asked.

The doctor held up her hairy paw. "Scout's honor, I promise. But please, please hurry!"

"Okay, let's get going," Sean said. "We need to take

you to another doctor friend of ours!"

FRIDAY, 19:14 PDST

By Friday evening, everything had returned to normal in Midvale. Even Jeremiah was acting normal . . . well, for Jeremiah.

Sean and Melissa were busy watching TV while Dad read the evening newspaper. The Channel 34 News was on the air, featuring—who else?—Rafael Ruelas. He stood next to Coach Nelson in the Midvale High School locker room. Behind them, several Midvale football players jumped around, shouting and clowning for the camera.

"This is Rafael Ruelas reporting live from Midvale High School, where the Midvale Tigers are about to play their third football game of the season. The Tigers haven't won a game yet, but that seems likely to change tonight. Right, Coach?"

"That's right, Rafael! Now that we know this curse thing was all a bunch of foolishness . . . well, the boys are all fired up and ready to go!"

Rafael nodded and turned back to the camera. "As you know, I've been saying all along that there's no such thing as a curse. And the fact that a lot of people actually believed in it just goes to show you how silly some folks can be!"

"Can you believe this guy?" Sean asked.

"He never ceases to amaze me," Melissa agreed.

The Midvale players continued jumping up and down as they prepared to take the field. Coach Nelson turned and shouted to them, "Okay, men, go out there and win one for dear old Midvale!"

"WIN . . . FIGHT . . . DESTROY!" they yelled as they ran for the door leading out to the field. The TV camera followed the first player through the door . . . until he tripped and fell on his face, causing the rest of the team behind him to pile up and collapse like dominoes.

"Oh no," Sean groaned.

"The Midvale Tigers aren't cursed," Melissa said. "They're just clumsy!"

Dad looked up from his paper. "It says here that the National Association of Psychologists might take away Dr. Williams' license." Then, folding up the paper, he continued, "I hope you two know how proud I am of you for solving this case. And I hope we've all learned that God doesn't expect His kids to live in fear of curses, or anything else, for that matter."

Melissa nodded.

"And I've learned something else, too," Sean said. "I've learned to be happy with myself just the way I am. I don't need a beard or a . . . a . . . ah . . ." He threw back his head and . . .

AH-CHOOOOO!

. . . sneezed violently. As he did, giant clumps of hair began sprouting up all over him.

"Oh no!" he moaned. "Not again."

At that exact moment on TV, Rafael Ruelas walked forward, stepped into a puddle, and . . .

POOF!

. . . disappeared in a flash of light. When the smoke cleared, Jeremiah had once again taken his place.

"We have a saying in the sports world, folks," he said. "It ain't over till the skinny gentleman dances."

"Fat lady sings!" Sean corrected.

"So stay tuned," Jeremiah continued, "because these Midvale players can really move the old goatskin."

"Pigskin!" Sean shouted at the screen.

Melissa sighed and turned to her brother. "I have a feeling it's going to be a long, long season."

"I'm afraid so," Sean nodded sadly while giving a good scratch under his furry armpits. "Say," he asked, "does anybody have some flea powder?"

By Bill Myers

Children's Series:
Bloodhounds, Inc. — mystery/comedy
McGee and Me! — book and video
The Incredible Worlds of Wally McDoogle — comedy

Teen Series:
Forbidden Doors

Adult Novels:
Blood of Heaven
Threshold
Fire of Heaven
Eli

Nonfiction:
Christ B.C.
The Dark Side of the Supernatural
Hot Topics, Tough Questions
Faith Encounter

Picture Books:
Baseball for Breakfast

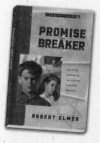